I0549407

RAMBLIN' RED

Michael *Easterling*

Other books by Michael Easterling

The Water at the End of the World

Christmas Eve on the Underground Railroad
    and Other Christmas Stories

Sweet Hope: an Appalachian Ghost Story

Jasper

Copyright © 2020 Michael Easterling
Cover art by Russ Flint
All rights reserved.
ISBN: 978-1-7344339-0-6

 VALLEY OAK PUBLICATIONS

To Sharon,
who teaches me kindness.

Chapter 1

Ramblin' Red leaned forward, resting his forearms on the horn of his saddle as he stared down the main street of Pandemonium.

"What do you think, Cricket?" he said. "Do things look right to you?"

Cricket, Ramblin' Red's horse and faithful companion, answered by shaking his head, sending a cloud of dust into the still, dry air.

The town of Pandemonium, New Mexico should have appeared as wild and unruly as its name implied. Now the streets lay deserted. No cowboys brawled in the streets; no tipsy idlers stood by, looking on; no children ran in and out among the harried housewives hurrying to do their late afternoon shopping. Even the ever-present dogs had abandoned the town square where they usually took their siesta in the shade of the age-old cottonwood tree.

Ramblin' Red took off his hat and scratched his head. Save for the absence of people and dogs, the town looked the same. Signs on storefronts continued to announce the nature of the businesses therein; hitching rails anticipated the visitation of horses; empty kegs, lining the boardwalk, waited to be sat upon. Even bright red geraniums beckoned cheerily from the window box of the dressmaker's shop. But as for people, there were none. Pandemonium looked as if some vile scourge had descended upon it, forcing its inhabitants to flee and to leave everything behind.

Ramblin' Red put his hat back on. "I do believe, Cricket, we best proceed with caution."

He guided Cricket over toward the saloon where he dismounted, not bothering to tie the reins to the post.

"Might be we'll have to leave this here town pronto," he explained to Cricket in a low voice.

The tramp of his boot heels as he stepped up onto the boardwalk seemed a violation of the Sabbath stillness. Cautiously, he swung open the saloon's swinging doors. The saloon, too, was empty. That the inhabitants had departed hurriedly was evident by the overturned chairs, the glasses of whiskey left untouched, the bartender's cleaning rag dripping water down the side of the bar.

Ramblin' Red picked up a glass of whiskey, tilted his head back, and flung the amber liquid back against his tonsils. As he wiped his mouth with the back of his hand, a voice called out from the street.

"Sheriff?"

Silence.

"Sheriff, do you hear me? I'm calling you out, Sheriff."

Ramblin' Red moved to the swinging doors and looked out over them. Standing in the street was a man neither short nor tall, fat nor thin. Only two things distinguished the man's appearance. First was his fancy garb, which included a gambler's satin vest, a bowler perched rakishly upon his head, and pearl-handled six-shooters set in holsters low upon his hips. Second was the nasty smirk on the man's face, which Ramblin' Red instinctively wanted to slap off. Even without having seen the "wanted" posters, Ramblin' Red would have known the man in the street, for he and Kid Torkasky had had dealings in the past, and the memory of them made Ramblin' Red's trigger fingers twitch.

"Sheriff, do you hear me?" the Kid called out again.

From a nearby alley way emerged Sheriff Frank Roswell. "I hear you, Kid," the sheriff said.

Ramblin' Red only knew Sheriff Roswell by sight, but had heard of the sheriff's reputation for being hard working, fair-minded and courageous—obviously far more courageous than the rest of the town residents who appeared to have abandoned the sheriff to face the Kid alone.

"I'm calling you out, Sheriff," the Kid cried. "What do you say to that?"

Sheriff Roswell stepped out into the middle of the street and faced the Kid. "Well, Kid, here I am."

Ramblin' Red knew of Kid Torkasky's fearsome reputation as a gunslinger. He also knew it to be total hogwash. If the Kid had ever killed anyone it was by shooting him in the back, either that or in an ambush by himself or with one of his no-good henchmen. For the Kid to be now confronting Sheriff Roswell face-to-face meant some manner of treachery had to be in play.

Ramblin' Red picked up an empty whiskey bottle and stumbled out into the street. "Hey, Bartender," Ramblin' Red cried, waving the bottle and reeling like a drunkard, "give me some more whiskey!"

Without taking his eyes off the Kid, Sheriff Roswell waved Ramblin' Red back. "Get off the street, cowboy. I don't want anybody getting hurt."

Ramblin' Red turned to obey, but in turning, he glimpsed a man sighting a rifle out of a second-story window of the hotel across the street. Turning further, he saw another rifle barrel protruding out over the false front of the hardware store opposite. Ramblin' Red knew that as soon as Sheriff Roswell went to draw his pistol, he was going to be cut down in a deadly crossfire.

There are animals whose senses are far more acute than those of humans. Eagles, for instance, soaring high in the sky, can see the tiniest, earthbound rodent that no human could possibly see from such heights. Likely there are other animals that can see quickness of speed that no human eye can detect. Such an animal might have seen what happened next, for surely no human could have. Spinning, Ramblin' Red drew his six-shooter from his holster, fired once through the hotel window, then directly through the false front of the hardware store. It all happened so blindingly fast, Ramblin' Red had already re-holstered his pistol before the man in the hotel, shot in the chest, gave out a scream. The result of Ramblin' Red's second shot was far more dramatic. The man atop the hardware store tumbled over the store's short false front, landed with a bang upon the corrugated metal of the store's porch roof, rolled three times down that slope and flopped down onto the dusty street, dead. Both Sheriff Roswell and Kid Torkasky stood with mouths agape.

Ramblin' Red lifted his hat and saluted the sheriff. "Just thought I'd even things up a mite, Sheriff. Now you two can go right on ahead."

Roswell nodded his appreciation then turned again to face the Kid. "Okay, Kid, make your move!"

Kid Torkasky licked his lips. "Well now, Sheriff, I dunno." The Kid stumbled back a few steps, nearly tripping over his own feet. "I was just joking, you know. I mean, I wasn't really gonna shoot it out with you. I was just, uh…"

Sheriff Roswell brought one hand up toward the handle of his pistol. "You started this fight, Kid. Now, let's finish it."

In a panic, the Kid looked around for help, but anyone who might have come to his aid was dead. Realizing the hopelessness of any rescue, the famous gunslinger, Kid Torkasky, gave out a sigh, pushed his bowler back off his forehead, squared his shoulders, stood tall, and with the fastest move that he ever made in his life, turned tail and ran.

"Come back here!" the sheriff shouted, drawing his pistol. The sheriff didn't dare let the Kid escape, yet he was loath to shoot a man in the back. "Stop, Kid! Don't make me shoot!"

The Kid kept high tailing it out of town. The sheriff took aim and fired. The shot, about ten yards wide, plowed a furrow through the red geraniums of the dressmaker's window box. Roswell fired again, this time succeeding in punching a hole in the horse trough on the opposite side of the street.

Ramblin' Red rolled his eyes. No wonder the sheriff had a reputation for courage, for any man sworn to uphold the law who couldn't shoot straight surely had to be brave–or crazy. Ramblin' Red drew his pistol, timed his shot to coincide with that of the sheriff's and shot Kid Torkasky square in the…

Milton Mickelsen, the smallest and brightest student of William McKinley Middle School, sat at his classroom desk, studying what he had just written.

...and shot Kid Torkasky square in the...

What was the exact word he was searching for? "Ass?" Milton shook his head. Though Ramblin' Red a was hard-riding, straight-shooting cowboy, he was also a gentleman who hated to give offense in any way. That such a gentleman should use so crude a word as "ass" was unthinkable.

Milton tapped his front teeth with the eraser of his pencil. What about "rear end?" Somehow "rear end" sounded too much like a traffic accident, as if Kid Torkasky was rear ended by Ramblin' Red's bullet.

What about "*derrière?*" Milton started to write the word before realizing he didn't know how to spell it. Besides, Ramblin' Red would have been less likely to use a fancy French word than he would "ass."

...and shot Kid Torkasky square in the...

Katie Larsen, who sat directly behind Milton, gave Milton's chair a hard kick. Looking up, Milton saw Miss Droshky, his science and math teacher, waving a blackboard eraser to get his attention.

"Ah, Mr. Mickelsen, so nice of you to join us. Perhaps if you wouldn't mind leaving off your scribbling for a moment, you might name for us of one of the six simple machines."

"Lever, pulley, wheel and axle, wedge, inclined plane, and screw," Milton answered.

"Thank you, Milton, but I recall only asking for one."

Milton continued. "Each of these simple machines gives the user a definite mechanical advantage."

"True, Milton, but you're getting ahead of us."

"In a lever system," Milton went on, "the mechanical advantage is the length of the force arm divided by the length of the load arm."

"That's enough, Milton."

"Thus, you can lift a hundred kilograms of load with only twenty-five kilograms of force if the force arm is four times longer than the—"

"I said, enough!"

Rudy Kastorsky, seated in the row to the right, bounced a crumpled piece of paper off Milton's head. "Yeah, Mickelsen, shut up!" The other students laughed.

"All right, Rudy," Miss Droshky said, "that's enough of that. Now class, since our learned friend has just named for us one of the six simple machines, can someone else name another?"

No hands went up.

"Katie?" Miss Droshky said.

"A pulley, Miss Droshky."

"Very good." Miss Droshky looked around the classroom. "Anyone else?"

No one volunteered an answer even though Milton had just spoken them. Milton shook his head and went back to his word problem.

…and shot Kid Torkasky square in the…

"Buttock!" he yelled.

Heads turned as one to stare at Milton. Then the class erupted into laughter.

Miss Droshky, seeking to restore order, rapped her knuckles on her desk. "Class! Class!"

She was saved by the lunch bell ringing.

"Don't forget the homework assignment!" Miss Droshky shouted above the clamor of desk chairs being pushed back. "Mr. Mickelsen, stay put. You'll serve detention by staying in at lunch."

Rudy Kastorsky, sauntering past, slapped Milton in the back of the head. "Buttock!" he said, laughing.

Chapter 2

When the classroom had emptied, Milton returned to his writing. "None of that," Miss Droshky said. "Put your pencil away and your head down on your desk."

Milton obeyed, resting his forehead on his hands. He didn't mind all that much staying in at lunch. Better here than the lunchroom where he was constantly the butt of some joke about how short he was, or where the best part of his lunch was often stolen when the lunchroom monitor wasn't looking. He regretted, however, that Miss Droshky wouldn't let him write, for he much preferred the world of Ramblin' Red to that of his own. Of course, back in Ramblin' Red's time, Milton's outburst of "buttock" likely would have earned him a "whupping," but Milton gladly would have suffered a whupping for a chance to live in the Old West. Besides, he was sure his teacher would have been a young, pretty schoolmarm who, unlike Miss Droshky, would have actually *liked* Milton and rather than wishing to punish him, would have encouraged him in his writing.

He looked up and stared at Miss Droshky. In one hand, she held a chocolate cupcake, and in the other one of those "bodice rippers" she was forever reading. Milton stared at the cover, which showed a helpless redhead in the arms of a bare-chested hunk while ocean waves crashed on the sandy beach behind them.

What drivel! he thought. What insipid escapism! Which posed the question of what Miss Droshky was trying to escape from? Perhaps from her students, for she seemed not to like them very much. He certainly knew Miss Droshky didn't like him. Well, the feeling was mutual!

Milton sighed. If only he could have lived in the Old West…

"You're a tough little nut," the red-faced schoolmarm, Miss Droshky said, holding another broken hickory switch, the third she'd broken while lashing Milton across his buttock.

Though the pain was excruciating, Milton wasn't about to give Miss Droshky the satisfaction of seeing him cry. "Will that be all, Miss Droshky?"

"No that will not be all, you impertinent brat!"

Milton gave her a self-satisfied smile. "Actually, Miss Droshky I think 'impudent' would be a better word choice. 'Impertinent' implies irrelevance, although I guess–"

"Silence!" Miss Droshky yelled. "Just for that, you will write 'impertinent' one thousand times on the blackboard!" Miss Droshky tossed the broken stick aside and began to pull on black riding gloves. "As for me, I shall go for a ride in the country, and when I return, you best be done." Turning on her heel, Miss Droshky strode out of the classroom and down the steps to where a horse and wagon awaited her.

Skirting the town of Pandemonium, which she had always considered a blight upon the landscape, Miss Droshky followed the road that led up onto the mesa, which offered glimpses down into the Pecos River canyon. A golden eagle, riding a warm current of air, soared in lazy circles above her, while white clouds, like majestic sailing ships, floated across the sea-blue sky. With a sigh, Miss Droshky let the beauty of the landscape ease her over-strung nerves and gave herself over to the pleasure of thinking up new ways she might torment Milton Mickelsen.

Had she not been so relaxed, Miss Droshky might have kept control of the reins and thereby saved herself. As it was, when the rattlesnake gave its warning rattle, the horse bolted, tearing the reins from her hands. All she could do was grip the wooden seat and plead for the horse to stop.

"Whoa, horsey! Whoa!"

But the horse, mad with fear, raced along the road as if chased by a pack of slavering hellhounds. With no rider to direct this wild chase, the horse continued straight on at the bend in the road and out across the open mesa. Over the rocky terrain the wagon leaped about like spit on a hot griddle, causing Miss Droshky to be ejected from her seat in a half somersault that landed her face down in the wagon bed.

"Ugh!" she exclaimed as the wind was knocked out of her. The wagon continued to leap about. In desperation, Miss Droshky tore her finger nails, trying to grip the wagon bed's rough planking, but with each bounce, she was thrown further and further back on the wagon bed until her legs were dangling off the open end.

"Whoa, horsey! Please, horsey!"

From her precarious position, she could not see the horse, which might have been just as well, for it was headed straight toward the mesa's rim and a plunge into the canyon below. Another bump and Miss Droshky was bounced even further back until only her fingers gripped the tailgate as the rest of her waved behind the wagon like a streamer blowing in the wind.

"Whoa! Whoa, you stupid, old nag!"

Perhaps this insult penetrated the horse's panicked brain, for at that moment, the horse saw its predicament. With scant feet from the mesa's edge, the horse saved itself by wheeling right. The wagon also was saved, though its back wheels swung out over the cliff. Miss Droshky, who was forever reprimanding her students for playing the potentially injurious game of "crack the whip," was about to learn first-hand the reason why. With a crack like a rifle shot, Miss Droshky, screaming, was rocketed out over–"

"Milton Mickelsen!"

Milton blinked to clear his vision and saw Miss Droshky, one hand pressed against her chest, staring wide-eyed at him. "Why are you looking at me like that?"

"Like what?"

"Like you're hurling knives out of your eyes!"

Milton shook his head. "Sorry, I was just thinking of a story."

She pointed toward the open door. "Well, go think somewhere else." She shivered. "I swear, sometimes you give me the creeps!"

Chapter 3

Milton took his accustomed seat next to Katie Larsen on the school bus. He could tell she was mad at him.

"What did I do now?"

"You know what you did. Miss Droshky asked you a simple question and then you go rattling on and on as if you know everything."

"I can't help it. I get bored."

"Well, how am I supposed to feel reciting an answer you've just given? It makes me feel like a talking parrot. It's stupid!"

"I'm sorry."

Katie turned to stare out the window. She still looked mad. But then she smiled and began to laugh. "'Buttock'? What was that about?"

Milton hung his head. "I was having trouble finding the right word for the story I'm writing." He went on to explain about Ramblin' Red shooting Kid Torkasky.

"Well, you don't have to blurt it out like that. Especially a word like 'buttock.' It makes you sound like an idiot."

"Tell me about it. Rudy must've called me 'buttock' ten times already."

The bus began to slow for Katie's stop.

"Are you still mad at me?" Milton said.

"Of course not," she said, slipping past him. Then she leaned over and whispered into his ear. "Buttock!" They both laughed.

Milton always felt a little sad to see Katie go, for he saw too little of his friend. Indian Falls, where Milton had recently moved with his grandmother, was a small mountain town surrounded by hundreds of square miles of National Forest. Most of the residents did not live in town, but on private parcels scattered along the main highway. The cabin of Milton's grandmother was the last stop on the bus route, more than ten miles out of town and six miles past Katie's house.

When the last student other than himself had been dropped off, Milton moved forward to sit behind Mr. Cunningham, the bus driver. Besides Katie, Mr. Cunningham was his only other friend. At first, Milton did not speak to Mr. Cunningham, except to say hello and goodbye. Then one day, Milton saw Mr. Cunningham at the celebration of Pioneer Days, an annual event in the town of Indian Falls. Milton hardly recognized the bus driver, for Mr. Cunningham was outfitted as a mountain man in hand-sewn moccasins, beaded buckskins, and a genuine beaver skin hat. Sitting on an Indian blanket, Mr. Cunningham demonstrated to his audience how to bait a trap with animal musk; how to load a rifle using a powder horn, wadding and a ball of lead; how to cast that ball of lead using a crucible and a mold. He displayed a canteen he had made from a gourd, and skins he tanned and cured, using nothing but a skinning knife and tannin from an oak tree.

When the talk ended, Milton stayed on, asking questions. Pleased by Milton's interest, Mr. Cunningham showed Milton how to start a fire using flint and steel. It was more than just the wood shavings that were ignited when Milton succeeded. Something inside him was fired as well; he felt empowered by his ability to make one of man's basic necessities.

From that beginning, a friendship grew. In response to Milton's wanting to know more about mountain men, Mr. Cunningham introduced him to the novels of A.B. Guthrie Jr., Irving Stone, and Vardis Fisher, which led Mr. Cunningham to share with Milton his other favorite genre of literature: westerns. It wasn't long before Milton was addicted to the works of Max Brand, Zane Grey, S. Omar Barker and Jack Schaefer.

"How's Ramblin' Red doing today?" Mr. Cunningham said.

Milton had shared several of his stories with Mr. Cunningham. "Great! He just saved Sheriff Roswell from getting killed by Kid Torkasky and his gang."

Mr. Cunningham looked at Milton in his rear-view mirror. "Do I sense some similarity between Kid Torkasky and our own Rudy Kastorsky?"

Milton grinned. "Maybe."

Mr. Cunningham halted the bus at Milton's stop then turned in his seat. "So what happens next?"

"Well, I'm thinking I'm going to need a reason for Ramblin' Red to stay in the town of Pandemonium and not go rambling off. I was thinking about a contest with one hundred dollars as first prize."

Mr. Cunningham whistled. "A hundred dollars was a lot of money back when a dollar a day was considered a good wage. So, what kind of contest?"

"I don't know yet, but something tells me it should have three events."

"Three is always a good number."

"I was thinking of maybe a horse race and a shooting contest, but I haven't figured what the third event should be. Any suggestions?"

Mr. Cunningham scratched his chin. "I can think of a few. Back in the days of the mountain men, when they would get together at the yearly rendezvous, they'd have all sorts of contests, like wrestling matches to see who was the best fighter. Sometimes those matches turned pretty violent."

Milton shook his head. "I can't see Ramblin' Red having to prove himself the best fighter. He would only use force if absolutely necessary."

Mr. Cunningham nodded. "Well, Ramblin' Red is a cowboy, so–"

"I know! There could be one of those steer-roping contests like in a rodeo." Milton stood up and picked up his backpack. "Talking to you always gives me good ideas."

Mr. Cunningham smiled. "Glad to help." He pulled the handle that opened the bus door. "Ramblin' Red will win the contest, of course."

"Of course," Milton said, as he skipped down the steps.

"Keep your powder dry, Milton," Mr. Cunningham said.

Milton turned and gave the practiced response. "Watch your top knot, and I'll watch mine."

Chapter 4

As Milton ambled up the driveway to his grandmother's house, set back in the woods, he thought about Ramblin' Red. As of yet, he had no details concerning the contest, but that did not bother him, for often he did not know where a story was going until he actually sat down to write it. Writing for him was like one of those scenes in the old movies where the boss is dictating a letter to his secretary. In Milton's case, the boss was a little man inside Milton's head, telling a story, and it was Milton's job, as secretary, to write it down. Sometimes the little man dictated something completely unexpected, as if he were truly someone with his own thoughts.

Milton had given the little man inside his head a name: Walt. Yet if asked to describe Walt, Milton would have been at a loss, for Walt had no face, nor age, nor personality. He was just a voice, though Milton could not have described that voice either. Yet whenever Milton was troubled by school, or worried about whether he would ever grow taller, or just having a hard time falling asleep, Walt would always be there to tell him a story, to take him away from the world the way it was, to the world as he would like it to be.

In fact, Walt was trying to tell him something right now, something to do with Ramblin' Red and the contest. Walt, however, was interrupted by the sound of spraying gravel. Milton jumped off to the side as Marta, his grandmother, brought her old pick-up truck to a stop beside him.

"I'm going to town," she called. "Care to come along?"

Milton ran around to the other side of the truck and got in.

"How was school?" Marta said, as she drove out onto the highway.

"Fine," Milton lied. Milton knew his grandmother worried about how he was adjusting to his new school, yet he felt he should deal with any problems on his own. It's what Ramblin' Red would have done.

But his grandmother was not fooled. "I know it's hard changing schools, but I think you'll find a small school better in the long run. I just couldn't stand to see you swallowed up in that big school back in the city."

Milton did not want to argue, but could not keep from saying something. "But a big school has so much more to offer, like advanced placement classes, and electives. What about my writers' club? There's nothing like that at McKinley."

"Well, why don't you start one?"

"With whom? Other than Katie, I don't think anyone else can even read, let alone write. They're all a bunch of jocks."

"Well, take up a sport then."

"Yeah, like I'm such an athlete."

His grandmother changed the subject. "I've got a few things to pick up at the store. Then how about a hamburger and milkshake at Chubby's?"

Milton grinned. "You'll have strawberry, of course."

Milton knew Marta was allergic to strawberries. Without taking her eyes off the road, she landed a soft punch to Milton's arm.

It was a long way to Indian Falls and to amuse himself Milton tried to make sense of the numbers that were posted to identify the many logging roads they passed. But he soon grew tired of this and took his writing pad from his backpack.

"What have you been writing? Anything new?"

"Yes, I've started a new Ramblin' Red story. He just saved Sheriff Roswell's skin."

"Refresh my memory. Roswell is the sheriff of Pandemonium, right?"

"Right."

Marta chuckled. "I love that name, Pandemonium. It's perfect for a wild west town."

"I got it from that book you gave me." That book was *Paradise Lost* by John Milton, given in an attempt, Milton believed, to wean him away from westerns. With its archaic language and its allusions to classical mythology, Milton found *Paradise Lost* tough going, though he did enjoy the descriptions of the beasts that inhabited hell.

"You were named for John Milton, you know," Marta said. "Indirectly, anyway."

It was a story Milton had heard often. His great-grandfather had named his sons Shakespeare, Blake and Milton, after his favorite poets. In turn, Milton was named after his grandfather, the one who built the cabin he and his grandmother were now living in and who was killed in the same car accident that claimed the lives of Milton's parents back when he was just a toddler. Of the three names, Milton was certainly better than Shakespeare, but perhaps not as interesting as Blake.

Blake Mickelsen. Milton thought he might use it as a *nom de plume*. Then again, he could just imagine someone like Rudy Kastorsky calling him "Blake the Flake."

"Why don't you read me what you've written," Marta said. "Help keep me awake while I'm driving."

Milton read about Ramblin' Red, Sheriff Frank Roswell and Kid Torkasky.

"What do you think?" he said, when done.

"I think it's good," Marta answered, "considering the genre. I don't know about the phrase 'blindingly fast' though. It's a cliché I've never quite understood."

"What did you think about Ramblin' Red having to shoot the Kid because the sheriff is such a bad shot?"

Marta smiled. "You've always had a good sense of humor. I'd just watch putting too much of it into your writing."

"Why? People like reading funny things."

She glanced over at him. "You're a good writer Milton, and I think, in a way, better than a lot of those writers of westerns you're so fond of reading. I'm just glad you're writing westerns while you're so young, so you can get them out of your system."

"But westerns are great! And lots of people read them."

"Yes, and a lot of very good writers have written them. But I believe you have the potential to be a great writer."

"You're telling me A.B. Guthrie Jr. wasn't a great writer?"

"What I'm trying to say is that there are many good writers, but a great writer is someone who not only writes well, but writes about something worth writing about. That's why I caution you about trying to be too funny. I believe that's why Mark Twain failed to be a great writer; he just couldn't resist turning everything into a gag."

"But *Huckleberry Finn* is one of the greatest books of American literature!"

"I would say the first part of *Huckleberry Finn* is one of the greatest books. Then Tom Sawyer shows up and it's all pratfalls and slapstick again."

Milton turned to stare out the window as the first outbuildings of Indian Falls came into view.

Marta reached over and patted his leg. "Don't worry. Someday you'll find your true writing voice. What's important is that you're writing and doing a good job."

"I still think *Huckleberry Finn* is a great book," he said.

Marta slowed to turn into the parking lot of the market. "Do you want to come in with me, or would you rather wander around town?"

Milton snorted. "That would take all of about two minutes." At one time, Indian Falls had been a thriving mill town with two active lumber mills. But the mill companies had decided it was cheaper to truck the timber down out of the mountains to a new, state-of-the-art lumber mill located down on the flats. Now Indian Falls survived by the presence of the National Forest Service and by the tourists who came to the mountains for recreation during the summer.

The only businesses which had not closed were the market, Chubby's restaurant, a hardware store, and a combination filling station and auto parts store.

Milton picked up his backpack. "I think I'll find someplace where I can do a little writing."

"Okay," Marta said. "Let's meet back here in about half an hour. Then we'll drive over to Chubby's."

Milton crossed the street and cut across the parking lot of the sheriff's office, housed in a large Quonset hut. The sheriff, who had just gotten out of his patrol car, walked over to Milton.

"I saw you getting out of Marta Mickelsen's pickup. Since you look a lot like her, I guess you must be related."

"Yes, sir," Milton said, "I'm her grandson."

"Well, I've known Marta since our days in the old one-room schoolhouse. If you're anything like her, you're a good person." He held out his hand. "I'm Matt Tulles, by the way."

Milton shook the sheriff's hand. "Milton Mickelsen."

"A pleasure to meet you, Milton. You tell Marta I said, hello, okay?"

Milton was pleased Sheriff Tulles had taken the time to introduce himself, and he thought the graying, somewhat rotund, sheriff was a lot like how he imagined Sheriff Frank Roswell. He found an old stone wall to sit on and took out his writing pad.

"I can't thank you enough for all your help," Sheriff Roswell said as he shook hands with Ramblin' Red.

Ramblin' Red was about to reply when interrupted by a sharp cry of distress. "Ow! I thought that stuff you gave me was supposed to keep me from hurting!"

Sheriff Roswell gestured toward the doctor's office from whence the complaint was issuing. "Can't say as I feel all that sorry for the Kid. He just better not give our new sawbones any trouble."

"Ow! Go easy will you, Doc!" Kid Torkasky yelled.

Ramblin' Red grinned. "One thing's for sure, the Kid won't be able to park his backside on a saddle anytime soon."

"No, siree," Sheriff Roswell said. "And with the number of warrants out on him, I reckon the Kid will be lucky if he gets less than twenty years in the pen."

Ramblin' Red started to gather up Cricket's reins.

"So, you're leaving?" the sheriff said. "I was hoping you might consider sticking around. What would you think about taking on a job as my deputy?"

Ramblin' Red swung himself up into the saddle. "I appreciate the offer, Sheriff, I truly do, but I'm afraid I'm not the 'sticking around' type."

"Well, that's a pity," the sheriff said, "because you'll miss the big contest. First prize is one hundred dollars."

Ramblin' Red practically leaped out of the saddle. "Did you say a hundred dollars?"

"Yep, to the man that can shoot the best, ride the best, and rope the best."

Ramblin' Red rubbed his chin. A man could work a whole season herding cattle and not make half as much as a hundred dollars. "What's a fella gotta do to get himself into this contest?"

"First off, he's gotta step over to Shorty's Saloon and pay the two-dollar entry fee. Then he's got to stick around until tomorrow when the contest begins."

Ramblin' Red grinned. "I guess I might be persuaded to stay that long." He looked down the long main street of Pandemonium. "By the way, which one of the saloons is Shorty's?"

Chapter 5

Milton had become so immersed in his writing, he had forgotten about the time. He shoved his writing pad into his backpack, jumped down off the wall and ran back toward the market. As he drew near, he saw an enormous bulldozer atop a parked trailer. Milton had a fascination with big machines, and he took time to examine this one. Though the outsides of the heavy steel treads of the bulldozer were worn shiny smooth, the insides were encrusted with dirt. Sadly, along with the dirt, were the remains of a gray squirrel, which had somehow gotten caught in the treads. It was only recognizable by the feathery tail, which was undamaged.

Milton wanted that tail. He wanted it to show to Mr. Cunningham. He wanted it to hang from the back of his ball cap. Grabbing onto the chain which anchored the bulldozer to the trailer, Milton began to pull himself up. He had just gotten one leg onto the bed when he was grabbed from behind and yanked back down.

"And just what do you think you're doing, squirt?" A giant of a man, dressed in grease-stained overalls towered over him. The man glared at Milton with eyes set so deep they looked like pits in his skull. "Messing with my tractor, are you?"

"No," Milton said, pointing, "There's a—"

Before Milton could get out another word, the man shoved him, and he fell hard upon his rump.

"Karl Kastorsky, how dare you!" Milton's grandmother, clutching two bags of groceries, stood looking on in anger.

Karl pointed down at Milton. "Does that little runt belong to you?"

"That boy is not a little runt. He's my grandson, and you've no right to treat him or anyone like that."

"Well, your puny grandson was trying to sabotage my dozer."

By this time, Milton had gotten himself up off the pavement. "That's not true! I was only trying to–"

"Hush, Milton," Marta said. She stepped forward until her grocery bags were pressing against Karl's chest. "My grandson does not sabotage dozers. My grandson is a good boy, so don't you ever treat him like that again!"

For several seconds Karl and Marta glared at each other. Then Karl broke into a grin. "You're a feisty, old bawd, Marta."

"And you've always been a big, ugly bully, Karl Kastorsky."

Turning toward Milton, Karl said, "Keep away from my stuff, kid." Then he got into the truck that pulled the bulldozer and started the engine.

Milton took one of the bags of groceries from his grandmother. "I really didn't think I was doing anything wrong, honest."

"I wouldn't worry about it. Karl just likes to bully people."

As they walked toward Marta's pickup, Milton said, "Does Karl Kastorsky have a son?"

"Two sons. One's in the army, I think. The other is about your age."

Marta and Milton got into the truck and placed the grocery bags on the seat between them.

"Grandma, what's a 'bawd'?"

Marta, about to start the car, stopped. "Is that what he called me?"

"He said you were a 'feisty, old bawd.'"

"That was a very nasty thing to say. Trust someone like Karl Kastorsky to say it." Then Marta looked at herself in her rearview mirror. "Old? Why, I'm not old!"

Chapter 6

"So, what do you think?" Katie said, looking up at the announcement posted on the wall in the hallway at school. "You think you'll enter?" Milton shook his head. "I don't know. I'm a fiction writer, not an essayist."

The poster read:

> The Association of School Superintendents is pleased to announce the 37th annual writing contest open to all students ages 12 to 15. This year's theme is "Why do I write?" Entries must be typewritten, double spaced, and no more than 500 words in length.
>
> Prizes to the winners:
>
> Grand Prize: $1,000 scholarship and a new Dell computer.
>
> 1st place: $750 scholarship.
>
> 2nd place: $500 scholarship.
>
> 3rd place: $250 scholarship.
>
> 4th–10th place winners will each receive a $100 gift certificate from Barnes and Noble.
>
> All entries must be postmarked no later than December 31st.

Rudy Kastorsky, who had sneaked up from behind, slapped Milton on the back of the head. "Hey, buttock, what're you staring at?"

"Quit calling him buttock!" Katie yelled.

Rudy grinned. "Sticking up for the squirt, are you, Katie–Matey?"

"Shut up, Rudy," Milton said.

Rudy shoved Milton up against the wall. "Who's gonna make me? You?"

Katie pushed her way between Milton and Rudy. "Leave him alone or I'll report you!"

"Oh, sure," Rudy said, "run to a teacher to save the little baby." But he stepped back from Milton and looked up to read the poster. "Ha!" he exclaimed. "You should write on why you like being a buttock. I'm sure you could write 500 words about that, Milton."

"You're just jealous because Milton has a talent for writing and you don't!" Katie said.

"Oh yeah, like I really want to waste my time scribbling on paper." He looked at Milton. "Why don't you learn to do something that takes real skill, like football? Our team could use someone your size." He began to walk away. "For the football!"

"What a jerk!" Milton muttered, rubbing the back of his head. "Has he always been like that?"

"No, not really," Katie said. "Rudy used to be really nice." She and Milton began to walk to their next class, science with the crabby Miss Droshky. "You know, he lost his mother a couple of years back?"

"Did he check the lost and found?"

Katie smiled. "It's not funny, really. She died of cancer, I think." She turned to look at Milton. "I guess you know what that's like, losing your parents."

Milton shrugged. "I barely remember them. I guess if I had been a little older it would have affected me more. All I really remember is growing up with Grandma."

Today's science lesson was on genetics, beginning with a lecture on the structure of DNA. Milton had learned all about genetics at his last school, so while Miss Droshky rattled on about nucleotides, base pairs, and the helix axis, Milton thought about the question the writing contest posed.

Why *did* he write? He was not sure it was something he could put into words. One reason he wrote was for something to do. Each day his social life ended when he got off the bus. He never watched television because his grandmother's cabin was too far out in the woods for television reception. It was the same problem with the computer Milton had brought with him from the city; his grandmother's house was too isolated to get internet service. About the only thing left to him, other than writing, was to read, which he did enjoy, but he had already read every western in the school library. Perhaps he should take his grandmother's suggestion and broaden his reading interests.

His desk shook as once again Katie had to kick it to get his attention.

He looked up to see Miss Droshky waving the blackboard eraser as if it were a signal flare. "Earth to Milton Mickelsen," she said.

Milton's face reddened as the other students laughed.

"Ah, I see you finally touched down," Miss Droshky said, obviously enjoying Milton's embarrassment. "While you were off-planet, we were talking about the four different nucleotides that make up DNA. Can you name one?"

"Adenine, guanine, cytosine, thymine."

"There you go again, getting ahead of us."

"These four nucleotides only differ in their nitrogenous base," Milton continued.

"That's more than enough, Milton."

"The structure of adenine consists of fifteen atoms: five carbon, five—"

A wad of paper bounced off Milton's head. "Shut up, Mickelsen," Rudy said.

Miss Droshky raised her voice to be heard above the laughter. "Milton, I sometimes wonder if you're hard of hearing. When I ask you to name one thing, I expect you to answer with just one. Now then class, since Milton has just named one of the nucleotides, can anyone else name another?"

No hands.

"Katie?"

Katie kicked Milton's chair hard before answering. "Guanine, Miss Droshky."

"Good. Anyone else?"

Silence.

Milton shook his head and returned to his musing, this time to Rudy's having lost his mother to cancer. Perhaps that had something to do with why Rudy was such a bully. Or maybe it was because he had a bully for a father. Maybe it was neither. Maybe Rudy was a bully because that's just the way he was. Milton liked this last idea best, for he was disinclined to harbor much sympathy for Rudy Kastorsky.

The idea of sympathizing reminded him of something Walt had started to tell him yesterday as he walked up his driveway, before his grandmother pulled up in her truck to take him to town. Walt had suggested that Ramblin' Red should lose the contest he was about to enter. Milton did not like this idea. He wanted Ramblin' Red to win, to triumph, to achieve fame and glory! Ramblin' Red was a hero not a loser! That said, Milton trusted Walt's instincts. Also, he was more than a little curious as to how Ramblin' Red's losing would play out.

When Miss Droshky turned to write on the blackboard, Milton silently slid his writing pad from his backpack.

The mayor of Pandemonium stood on a wagon bed where he could be heard and seen by everyone in the crowd. "Gentlemen, these are the rules. As you know, there are three events. The winner of each event will receive five points. Second place gets four points; third place, three, and so on. The man with the most points at the end of the day will be declared the winner and will receive the prize of one hundred dollars."

"What's the prize for second place?" said a cowboy who went by the name of Buck. Buck looked as if he had spent the night inside a whiskey bottle.

A short man with a tall hat answered. "A shot of my best whiskey." He motioned toward his saloon across the street. "Providing, of course, you got two bits."

This got a laugh from the crowd.

"What Shorty is saying," the mayor said, "is that this is a 'winner takes all' contest."

"What if there's a tie?" This from a dandified gentleman in a dark green suit with white lace around the wrists and collar.

"Then I reckon we'll have to have a run-off," the mayor said. "Now, if you gentlemen don't have any more questions, we'll get started with the day's first event, a horse race around the Needle and back!"

With much whooping, hollering, and waving of hats, the contestants rode their mounts down to the starting line, a rope stretching from a porch post on the Empire Hotel to the livery stable on the opposite side of the street. Getting all the contestants lined up took considerable time, for some of the horses shied away from such crowding, and more than one cowboy, already drunk, fell off his horse and had to be helped back on.

As Ramblin' Red waited for matters to sort themselves out, the man in the fancy green suit rode up and positioned his horse to the left of Cricket.

"Good morning," the man said, tipping his hat. "Nice day for a horse race." The man extended his hand. "The name's Nero Marceau."

Ramblin' Red reached across his saddle to shake hands. "I'm Max Schaefer, though most folks call me Ramblin' Red."

Nero glanced up at the red hair poking out from under Ramblin' Red's hat, but chose to comment instead upon Cricket. "That's a mighty nice looking pony you got there."

"I might say the same about yours."

Smiling, Nero reached forward to pat the neck of a black stallion that stood three hands higher than Cricket. "This fellow's name is Jupiter, and like me, he's Kentucky born."

Further conversation was prevented by the mayor signaling the race was about to begin. "Gentlemen, are you ready?" he said, pointing a pistol into the air.

"Good luck to you, Ramblin' Red," Nero said.

"Same to you, Nero."

The bang of the starting gun startled the horse to Ramblin' Red's right, and it was several seconds before Ramblin' Red could get clear of its bucking. By that time Nero and Jupiter were well out ahead. It didn't take long for Ramblin' Red to realize that he and Cricket were never going catch up to them. Though Cricket was the best little stock horse a cowboy could hope for, quick to cut out a cow from a herd, or run down a restless stray, he was no match for Jupiter, who had been bred for one thing: to run.

With no chance of winning, Ramblin' Red set his sights on second place. It soon became apparent he'd have competition from just one rider, Buck, the cowboy who had earlier asked about the prize for second place. Buck rode a sturdy mustang that looked to have great staying power. The same, however, could not be said of Buck. As the riders circled the Needle, a whittled spire of sedimentary rock pointing like an accusing finger skyward, the mustang boldly jumped a fallen timber, but its rider failed to follow. Ramblin' Red, who had been riding neck and neck with Buck, looked over his shoulder to see Buck pick himself up and immediately check the condition of a pint of whiskey stowed in his back pocket. With a grin, Buck waved the bottle to show that it hadn't broken. Ramblin' Red waved in return then looked ahead. No other rider separated him from Nero Marceau, and unless something unforeseen were to happen, Ramblin' Red was certain of a second-place finish.

What Ramblin' Red had no way of knowing was the determination of the man steadily closing the distance behind him. The rider was a young man, as broad and sturdy as Ramblin' Red was long and lean. He drove his poor horse mercilessly, jamming his boot heels hard into the horse's ribs and demanding more speed with stentorian curses. As the horse drew alongside Cricket,

Ramblin' Red saw blood trickling down the horse's side from where the rider's spurs had cut.

Ramblin' Red could not fathom how a man could abuse a horse in such a manner, even to win one hundred dollars. Well, he wasn't about to let such ill treatment go rewarded! With a yell, Ramblin' Red exhorted Cricket to a greater effort. But as he raised his leg to prod Cricket, the rider of the other horse leaned from his saddle and–

"Milton Mickelsen!" Miss Droshky yanked Milton's writing pad from under his pencil, causing the page to tear.

Milton was horrified. "Look what you've done!" Tears of rage and frustration welled up in his eyes.

Miss Droshky, for her part, looked contrite. "I'm sorry, Milton, I didn't mean for the page to tear." She ran a hand down the page, smoothing it out. "But it's your fault, really. This is a science class, and you've not been paying attention. It's not only disrespectful, it's rude."

Milton was tempted to point out the redundancy in her statement, but was afraid if he opened his mouth he might cry.

"From now on there'll be no more of your scribbling during my class." Miss Droshky walked back to her desk, taking Milton's writing pad with her. "You can get this back when class is over."

Chapter 7

Milton was mad enough to spit. In fact, he did, right on the blacktop of the playground.

"Oh, gross!" Katie exclaimed.

"That's for Miss Droshky taking my writing pad away; that's for her ripping up my work."

"She didn't rip it up. She only tore one page."

"I don't care! She had no right!"

"Well, it *is* kind of rude, your writing while everyone else has to sit and pay attention."

"I'm not 'everyone else.' I'm a writer, and I'm going to be a great one. The problem with Miss Droshky is she's jealous because she knows I've got talent and she doesn't."

Shaking her head, Katie began to walk away.

"Where you going?" Milton said.

Katie turned. "If I wanted to listen to a braggart, I'd hang out with Rudy."

Milton watched Katie go. He was sorry he had made her angry again. Sometimes he didn't know why he acted as he did, why he said things he knew were not true–that comment about Miss Droshky for instance; he didn't know what talents Miss Droshky had. As for him becoming a great writer, it was a dream, not a fact. It was just that, upon occasion, he felt the need to toot his own horn.

"The problem with being small," he muttered, "is that it makes you feel small."

Milton found an empty bench and took his writing pad from his backpack. In truth, little damage had been done to it. Everything but the last few words was legible. He got out a pencil and wrote over the hard-to-read words before continuing.

With a yell, Ramblin' Red exhorted Cricket to a greater effort. But as he raised his leg to prod Cricket, the rider of the other horse leaned from his saddle and yanked Ramblin' Red's boot out of his stirrup. The act was done with such deftness, doubtless no one watching from the finish line would have seen it. The effect upon Ramblin' Red was to throw him completely off balance. He had to cling to his saddle horn to keep from tumbling off Cricket. By the time Ramblin' Red got himself righted, the other horse was two lengths out in front and stayed there past the finish line.

The spectators cheered the exciting conclusion of the race, never suspecting what treachery had taken place. For his part, Ramblin' Red was furious. He meant to have "words" with the man who had chosen such an underhanded way to beat him. That man, however, had disappeared, and Ramblin' Red was too pressed upon by the throng of revelers to go in pursuit.

Ramblin' Red removed his hat and wiped the sweat from his forehead with the back of his hand. He would bide his time. But if it meant having to stay in Pandemonium for a whole month, he would find the man who tricked him. Such dirty dealing could not go unanswered!

Chapter 8

As Milton sat on the bus seat next to Katie, he felt her silence like a great stone wall between them. Finally, he could stand it no more. "I'm sorry," he said.

"You've said that before," she answered, gazing out the window.

Milton did not know what else to say. They continued to ride along in silence until Katie suddenly pointed. "Look!"

Milton leaned over Katie to look out the window. A doe and her two fawns were nibbling grass alongside the road.

"They're beautiful," Katie said.

Milton nodded. "Do you ever get out there much?"

Katie turned. "What do you mean?"

"Out there," Milton said, pointing toward the forest.

"Sometimes. My family does a lot of camping during the summer."

"There are a lot of logging roads out by our place, and I've walked down a few, but I've always been afraid to leave them in case I'd get lost, or run into a mountain lion or bear."

"I doubt you'd run into either," Katie said. "Still, I know what you mean."

"Sticking to the logging roads makes me feel like I'm in a zoo," Milton said. "I'm on one side of the fence and the wildlife on the other. I mean, I've spent my whole life in the city, and I know how to get around in it. But how do I get around out there?" He again pointed towards the forest.

"Maybe you should join the Boy Scouts or something." She gathered up her backpack as the bus began to slow for her stop.

"You still mad at me?"

"No. We're a lot alike, you know. I get bored, too." She stood up and slipped by him.

"See you tomorrow," Milton said.

"See you, O great writer."

A little later Milton once again moved forward to sit behind Mr. Cunningham.

"How's Ramblin' Red doing today?" Mr. Cunningham said.

Milton shrugged. "Okay, I guess."

"You guess?"

"My problem is I'm bored."

"You mean bored with Ramblin' Red, or bored in general."

"Bored in general. There's nothing to do around here!"

Mr. Cunningham brought the bus to a stop at Milton's driveway then turned in his seat. "What do you mean nothing to do?"

Mr. Cunningham looked a little angry, and for a moment, Milton was sorry he had said anything.

"Look around you, Milton! There's trees and woods to be explored. There are streams and lakes to fish and swim in. There are wild animals and birds waiting to be discovered."

"I know!" Milton exclaimed. "But how do I actually *do* that? I mean, even if my grandmother would let me, how do I explore all that out there without getting lost or maybe even killed?"

"Haven't you ever heard of backpacking?"

"I've *heard* of it; I've just never done any."

Mr. Cunningham ran his hand through his thinning hair. "Well, for Pete's sake." Mr. Cunningham turned the bus engine off and set the brake. "Come on!" he commanded, opening the bus door.

Milton grabbed his pack and ran after Mr. Cunningham up the driveway towards the cabin. "What are we doing?"

"We're going to talk to your grandmother."

As they drew near to the cabin, Milton ran ahead and opened the door. "Grandma!" he shouted.

Marta came from the kitchen, wiping her hands on a towel. Her look of concern changed to one of pleasure, seeing Mr. Cunningham standing behind Milton. "Jim Cunningham, how nice to see you!"

Mr. Cunningham smiled in return. "I heard you quit the city, Marta. About time, too."

"Wait a minute," Milton said. "You two know each other?"

Both Mr. Cunningham and Marta laughed. "Jim and I went to school together," Marta said.

"In the one-room schoolhouse?"

"Where did you hear about the one-room schoolhouse?"

"I met Sheriff Tulles yesterday, and he said you both were students at the one-room schoolhouse. It seems everybody knows you, Grandma."

"That comes from being raised in a small town," Marta said. "That's why I wanted us to move. Here we are part of a community. I never felt that way, living in the city."

"It seems though that our Milton finds our country ways a mite too slow," Mr. Cunningham said. "He's bored. That's why, if it's all right with you, I'd like to take him backpacking this weekend, show him there's no reason to be bored if you've got all this beautiful country to explore."

"Why I think that's a splendid idea," Marta said. "But isn't it getting to be a little late in the season?"

"Not really. I figure we got at least a month before the first snows. And we'll only be hiking up to Round Lake."

She turned to Milton. "You really want to go backpacking? It's probably going to be cold at night."

"Grandma," Milton replied, a big grin on his face, "I've been waiting my whole life to go backpacking."

Both Marta and Mr. Cunningham laughed.

"Well," Mr. Cunningham said, "I guess that settles it then."

"But Jim," Marta said, "I'm afraid a sleeping bag is about all I have in the way of camping gear."

"Not to worry. I got enough stuff to supply an army. All Milton will need, besides his sleeping bag, is a few personal items—clothes and such. I'll make a list for him." He turned to leave.

"Wait a minute, Jim. Would you like a cup of coffee?" Marta waved her towel toward the kitchen. "I got banana bread coming out of the oven."

"That's a tempting offer, Marta, but I got my bus parked in the road." He turned to Milton. "I'll have that list for you tomorrow. Then come Saturday, we'll try to do something about that boredom of yours."

Milton could no longer contain himself. Waving his arms, he jumped into the air. He thought of Ramblin' Red as he hollered. "Yee ha!"

Chapter 9

"All right, gentlemen," the mayor announced, "Here's how things stand so far. Nero Marceau, who came in first, now has the lead with five points. Randy Stark, who came in second, has four points; Ramblin' Red, three; Cass Layton, two; and Lucky Lars Skogland, one."

"What about me?" Buck said, standing before the mayor with thumbs tucked into his front pockets, a lopsided grin on his face.

"Well, what about you, Buck?" the mayor said.

"Well, I made it halfway around," Buck said. "That oughta be worth at least half a point."

The mayor turned to whisper something to Shorty, who, smiling, nodded in return. "Okay, Buck, a half-point for a half-wit."

This drew a laugh from the crowd. A few slapped Buck on the back, who, being of a good nature, did not appear at all offended by the mayor's gibe. While all this was going on, Ramblin' Red looked for Randy Stark, the man who had cheated him out of second place, but did not see him in the crowd.

"The rules of the shooting contest are simple," the mayor said, "and thanks to the saloon keepers, who've been saving empty bottles just for this occasion, we've got ourselves plenty of targets to shoot at. Each man gets one shot. If he hits the bottle, he goes onto the next round. If he misses, he's out of the contest. The man who stays in the longest is the winner."

"What if we run out of bottles?" Buck said.

"The way you've been drinking, Buck, that ain't likely."

"You should talk, Mayor!" someone shouted.

Grinning, the mayor pulled a bottle from his coat pocket and held it up. "I don't know what you mean. Why, this here bottle is almost–" The bottle exploded in his hand, showering him with whiskey. "Jumpin' Jehoshaphat!"

Nero Marceau lowered his rifle. "Sorry, mayor, but when you held that bottle up, I thought you were signaling for the contest to begin."

The crowd roared with laughter. The mayor, clearly shaken, pointed out to a distant mound of earth on which a row of bottles had been placed. "The targets are over there, you fool! Now, I'm getting out of here before I get killed!"

"Just a moment, Mayor!" Everyone turned to see who had spoken. A young woman in a lavender dress and a wide-brimmed straw hat stood, leaning upon a rifle. "Is this contest limited to men, or can a lady enter?"

The mayor scratched his head. "Well, I don't know. We ain't never had a lady ask before."

"I say, we let her compete," Nero shouted.

Others took up the cry. "Yes, give her a chance!"

"All right, then," the mayor responded. "But don't blame me if she winds up beating the pants off the lot of you."

An old board had been placed on the ground behind which the contestants were to stand while shooting. The row of bottles was one hundred paces out from the board. At such a distance, pistols, even in the hand of a crack shot like Ramblin' Red, were not nearly as accurate as rifles. Nero Marceau, having the most points in the contest, was allowed to go first. He competed with a custom-made Henry repeating rifle with an engraved barrel and a hand-carved butt stock. In one motion, he lifted the Henry to his shoulder, fired and blew the first bottle to smithereens. It was a sobering moment for all concerned. A few contestants turned away, deciding not to compete rather than be shown up. Not to be outdone, Ramblin' Red took aim with his Winchester single shot rifle and, just as he intended, knocked only the neck off the next bottle, leaving the remainder still standing.

"All right, gentlemen," the woman in lavender announced, "let's see if a lady can compete with you sharp shooters."

The mayor, who had decided not to go into hiding after all, spoke out. "No one would fault you, ma'am, should you decide to move a little closer to the target."

"Why, that's most chivalrous of you, Mayor," the lady answered as she sighted down her rifle barrel, "but right now I can't decide whether to shoot just one bottle or two."

The mayor snorted. "With just one shot?"

In response, the lady fired and hit a bottle on its edge, causing it to blowout sideways and shatter the two bottles next to it." The spectators were stunned into silence.

The lady, though, looked disappointed. "That was poor shooting. I had intended to only hit two bottles."

The mayor shook his head. "We just may run out of bottles after all!"

About thirty contestants followed, half of whom missed. Last to compete was Randy Stark. Ramblin' Red made note of Stark's sudden appearance, but decided the time was not right to confront him. Stark carried with him an old Springfield rifled musket.

"I've not seen one of those muskets since the War," Nero said.

"Where it saved my life on more than one occasion," Randy Stark answered, then lifted his musket to his shoulder, fired, and shattered a bottle.

There were many fine marksmen competing that day, but at the end of eight rounds, the field of contestants had been whittled down to just four: Ramblin' Red, Nero Marceau, Randy Stark, and the lady in lavender. It soon became evident that at the distance of just one hundred paces none of these were likely to miss, so it was decided to move the board back another one hundred paces.

"Would you gentlemen mind if I went first this time?" the lady in lavender said.

Ramblin' Red had noticed that, following her last two shots, the lady had winced in response to the recoil of her rifle. "We could delay this contest if you'd like to rest awhile."

The lady faced him. "Why, cowboy, those are the first words I've heard you speak today. I was beginning to think you might be dumb."

The twinkle of merriment in the lady's violet-blue eyes as she said this caused Ramblin' Red to smile. "I admit to lacking certain social graces–making polite conversation being one of them–but I don't believe I've ever been accused of failing to act kindly toward a lady, especially when she appears to be in pain."

The lady placed a hand upon her shoulder. "Yes, I shall be quite sore tomorrow. But I'd like one more shot, just to see if I can hit a target at that distance." The contestants moved aside to give her a clear shot. She was a long time sighting her rifle. Finally, she fired and missed. With a sigh, she lowered her rifle. "It looks like I need more practice."

"It was the wind," Nero said. "It perked up just before you shot." Ramblin' Red and Randy Stark nodded in agreement.

The lady drew a handkerchief from the sleeve of her dress, held it between two fingers then let it fall. It fell straight to the ground. "The air is dead calm, just as it has been all day. But thank you for your diplomacy."

The men tipped their hats as the lady departed. Then Ramblin' Red, seeing her handkerchief still upon the ground, sprang to pick it up. But as he held it up, he saw the lady had disappeared.

Grinning, Nero said, "I do believe she meant for you to have that." He turned toward the waiting line of bottles. "Now what say we finish this contest?"

The spectators were equally anxious for the contest to conclude, for the day had turned hot. In this, however, they were to be disappointed, for after a half a dozen more rounds, none of the contestants had missed his shot. It was then decided to move the board back another one hundred paces.

"Nobody can hit something that far away," a spectator observed. Others nodded in agreement, for the bottles seemed but specks in the distance.

"I've ten dollars that says I can," Nero said.

"You're on!" the spectator shouted back.

"You willing to make that bet with anyone, Nero?" someone else said.

Nero nodded. "I'll bet any man ten dollars, provided he's got the money to pay up." There was a flurry of activity as men got out their money. The mayor was elected collector, and the betting money placed in his hat.

"How about you two gentlemen?" Nero said, addressing Ramblin' Red and Randy Stark. "Care to make a friendly wager?"

Randy Stark shook his head. "Money is too hard to come by, and I'll not throw it away on a bet."

Nero turned to Ramblin' Red. "How about you, Ramblin' Red? Are you a gambling man?"

"I won't bet against, you, Nero. But I wager ten dollars I make my next shot."

Nero stroked his chin. "Likely I'm throwing my money away, but being a gambler by trade, I'll take that bet. Now which one of us wants to go first?"

"Might as well get this over with," Randy said. He carefully sighted along the barrel of his musket. "During the war, I once shot at a Rebel from this distance."

"I trust it was not one of my cousins," Nero said.

Randy slowly pulled back on the trigger, fired and missed. If Randy was disappointed, he didn't show it. "You'll be happy to know I didn't hit that Rebel either." He tucked his musket under his arm and disappeared into the crowd.

A sudden gust of wind kicked up the dust. Ramblin' Red and Nero looked at each other. Both realized that the wind would make it just that much harder to hit the target, and harder still should they delay and the wind grow stronger.

"You got more riding on this contest, Nero," Ramblin' Red said. "You go ahead and shoot next."

"Mighty kind of you." Like Randy Stark, Nero was a long time sighting his rifle. The bang of his rifle was followed by the sound of glass breaking. Groans went up in recognition of the money that had just been lost.

The wind was now blowing in gusts spaced about five seconds apart. Ramblin' Red felt confident of hitting his target, providing the wind did not do something funny, for an unexpected gust could cause the bullet to veer just enough to miss the target. He waited until a gust of wind subsided, counted to three then fired. The crowd cheered as once again there was sound of breaking glass.

Shorty, the saloonkeeper waved his hat to get attention. "I believe, gentlemen, that I speak for all when I say we've not seen better marksmanship than what has been demonstrated here today, so I'm going to offer an additional bonus to either man if he can make his next shot: a bottle of my best whiskey."

"Are you sure, Shorty?" the mayor said, "Think what'll happen if they both hit their next shot. You'll be out all of twenty cents!"

Shorty chased after the mayor, batting him with his hat, much to the delight of the crowd.

"The mayor has it right about the worth of Shorty's whiskey," Nero said to Ramblin' Red. "That said, I wouldn't mind wetting my whistle just now. So, let's hope one of us hurries up and misses." Nero raised his rifle, fired and shattered another bottle.

"I think you're going to have to stay thirsty awhile, Nero," Ramblin' Red said. He took aim, fired and another bottle disappeared.

It went on like that, neither man missing for several more rounds. In the excitement of the competition, the onlookers forgot about the hot sun. Before them was unfolding a story of unrivaled marksmanship, one that would be told and retold until one day it would reach the status of legend.

On his next shot, Nero took aim, fired and just nicked a bottle, causing it to wobble, but not break.

"Does that count?" someone said.

"It shouldn't!" someone else shouted.

Thereupon an argument broke out among the spectators as to whether Nero's shot should count or not. It didn't help matters that many were still sore about losing ten dollars to Nero. Heated words were spoken and several shoving matches broke out. A general melee was about to ensue when Ramblin' Red drew his pistol and fired into the air.

"Listen up!" Ramblin' Red shouted. He waited for two grappling men to be pulled apart. "You all heard what the mayor said when he laid out the rules. He said a man had to hit the bottle to go on to the next round. He didn't say anything about the bottle having to break. Now, you all saw, just as plain as day, that Nero hit the bottle, so his shot counts!" Ramblin' Red ran his eyes over the crowd, daring anyone to disagree. None did.

"Mayor, how much money you got in that hat of yours?" Nero said.

The mayor ran his fingers through the pile of bills. "Looks to be about two hundred dollars."

"Just so there's no hard feelings, I'm going to add that two hundred dollars to today's winner's take, and since I'll not be competing in the next event..." he ran a hand down the front of his expensive suit coat to show that he was not about to dirty his fancy duds, attempting to rope a steer, "that somebody won't be me."

"That's might good of you," Ramblin' Red told Nero, as the crowd cheered.

Nero grinned. "It's just a little business sense. I'll win it all back at the gambling tables tonight."

When the crowd quieted, Ramblin' Red prepared to take his next shot. The gusts of wind, though growing stronger, had still been coming steadily at about once every five seconds. Again, Ramblin' Red waited for the wind to subside before firing. But just as he pulled the trigger, a rogue gust, stronger than the others, blew hard across the ground that separated Ramblin' Red from the target. The gust was sufficient to change the trajectory of the bullet.

Ramblin' Red missed.

Chapter 10

"Now this is what you might call a vintage backpack," Mr. Cunningham said, holding it up so Milton could slip his arms through the shoulder straps. "It's the one I used back when I was about your age. Believe it or not, I wasn't much bigger than you are."

Milton liked that he was going to be using Mr. Cunningham's old backpack. He liked old things, things with a history. "So, all my stuff gets stuffed inside it?"

"Well, let's think about this a minute. When you're backpacking, you want your center of balance to be low. If your pack is too top heavy, you'll feel off balance." Mr. Cunningham lifted two black plastic containers out of the bed of his pickup truck.

"What're those?" Milton said.

"They're bear canisters for storing our food. They're designed to keep the food in and the bears out."

Hearing the word 'bear' sent a chill down Milton's spine. "Are we going to see any bears?"

"It's not likely, especially on a well-used trail like this," he said, pointing to the sign which marked the beginning of the trail to Round Lake. "Remember bears are more afraid of us than we are of them. Also, bears are usually nocturnal creatures, and it's at nighttime when the bear canisters really come in handy. Should a bear happen to stumble upon them, he'll be unable to open them up and steal our food."

"What about mountain lions?"

"What about them?"

"Will we see any?"

"I've been exploring these mountains most all my life, and I've only seen a mountain lion once. They're very secretive, and like the bear, nocturnal–even more so. If we're fortunate enough to see a mountain lion, we'll stand our ground and wave our arms or maybe a stick until he goes away." Mr. Cunningham placed one of the bear canisters in Milton's backpack. "Usually your trip food is the heaviest thing you'll carry, especially if you're going to be gone for many days."

"What's the longest backpacking trip you've ever been on?"

"I once hiked the John Muir trail, which is over two hundred miles."

"Wow! How long did that take?"

"I wasn't in any hurry, so I guess I was out about twenty days."

"And you carried all the food you needed?"

Mr. Cunningham shook his head. "I went in ahead of time and cached food in two places." He picked up Milton's sleeping bag. "Now we'll load the next heaviest thing." Milton's sleeping bag was thick, oversized, and rolled up and tied with string rather than stuffed into a stuff sack. "Is this the only sleeping bag you have?"

"We've got a smaller one, but grandma wanted to make sure I stayed warm."

"Well, it'll do for this trip, but the next time we'll find something lighter. Heavier doesn't necessarily mean warmer." Mr. Cunningham crammed the sleeping bag into Milton's backpack. It was so big, it almost filled up the entire space. "Looks like you got just enough room to pack the clothes I told you to bring."

Milton took off his backpack and stuffed his clothes in beside the sleeping bag. While he was doing that, Mr. Cunningham set three other items next to him: a water bottle, a small first aid kit, and a hatchet. "Those first two will fit in the pouches on the outside of your pack."

Milton lifted the hatchet, which was surprisingly lightweight. "I get to carry the hatchet?"

"So long as you're careful." He showed Milton where to hang the hatchet on a loop sewn into the backpack. "Okay, you're loaded up. Go ahead and put your backpack back on."

The backpack was heavy, but not uncomfortably so. Mr. Cunningham showed Milton how to adjust the straps so that the weight was mostly upon his hips. Then he put on his own backpack.

"Okay, we're ready to go." He pointed to the trailhead sign, which read: Round Lake – 3½ miles. "You lead the way."

"Cool!" Milton said, as he started up the trail.

"That way if we run into a bear, he'll eat you first," Mr. Cunningham said.

Milton spun around and saw Mr. Cunningham grinning.

"I mean, that way I'll know where you are."

The first part of the trail was mostly level. The air beneath the trees was chill, for though the sun was well up, little of its warmth penetrated the thick branches of the conifers. After a few minutes walking, however, Milton was beginning to sweat. It was a good sweat, not like in PE where he mostly chased after the other players who generally ignored him during play. Backpacking, Milton realized, was a recreation that didn't require a lot of other people or being super athletic; it was just him and his backpack, and consequently he felt it was something he could succeed in doing.

"Hold up there a second, Milton." Mr. Cunningham said in low voice.

Milton turned. "What is it?"

"Listen!"

Milton stood still and listened. He heard a tapping sound that even he, unversed as he was in the ways of the woods, could identify. "It's just a woodpecker."

"Not *just*," Mr. Cunningham answered. "Set down your pack and follow me." Mr. Cunningham removed his own pack then stepped off the trail and into the woods, trying to make as little noise as possible. Following the direction of the sound, they came to a place where a huge pine tree had fallen, taking several other trees down with it. Rays of sunlight streamed down through the gap in the trees, warming the dark soil. Mr. Cunningham sat down on one of the fallen logs and motioned for Milton to do the same. "He's very close by," Mr. Cunningham whispered.

"What are we looking for?" Milton whispered back.

"You'll see."

They did not have long to wait. First there was a bird call, rising and falling: *wuck-a-wuck-a-wuck*. Then a large bird flew into the top of a standing dead pine not more than fifty feet from them. It was, as Milton thought, a woodpecker, but unlike any woodpecker he had ever seen.

"What is it?" Milton said in a whisper.

"It's a pileated woodpecker," Mr. Cunningham whispered back.

The woodpecker was huge, nearly seventeen inches from its wedge-shaped tail to the brilliant red feathers of its pointed topknot. As Milton and Mr. Cunningham watched, the pileated woodpecker circled the tree, gripping it with its sharp talons. It hammered away at the dead wood, sending out a spray of wood chips.

Milton marveled that a bird, even one so large, could strike the tree with such force–and so rapidly, *rat-a-tat-tat!* like the rattle of a machine gun.

"What's it going after?" Milton said.

"Probably carpenter ants. That's what it usually eats."

They watched for several minutes as the pileated woodpecker continued to circle the tree, searching for ants. Then with a *wuck-a-wuck-a-wuck*, it flew off into the forest.

Mr. Cunningham stood up and dusted off the seat of his pants. "Well, that was certainly a sight worth seeing."

"Are pileated woodpeckers rare?"

"I wouldn't say rare, but you don't see them as often as other woodpeckers. I suspect a woodpecker that size needs a larger territory."

"How did you know it was a pileated woodpecker when we were back on the trail?"

"By the loudness of its pecking–much louder than other woodpeckers. Speaking of the trail, can you lead us back to it?"

Milton looked around. "I think we came that way," he answered, pointing, "but I'm not absolutely sure."

"Which direction was the sun when we left the trail?"

Milton closed his eyes, trying to remember. "I remember the sun was in my eyes as we walked." He opened his eyes. The sun was directly behind him. "So, I was right. The trail *is* back that way."

"Okay," Mr. Cunningham said, "lead on."

Milton stepped over the fallen logs and set a course through the woods. He came upon the trail not far from where they had left their backpacks.

"Good navigating," Mr. Cunningham said.

"That was easy," Milton said, lifting his backpack onto his shoulders. "But what would we have done if we had gone deeper into the woods, or maybe got turned around, or been gone so long the sun was in a different place?"

"If it had been a situation where there was a chance of us getting lost, we could've used the hatchet to make blaze marks on the trees to show us the way back, though I don't like to scar the trees. The best thing, if you're going cross country away from a trail, is to use a map and compass."

"That sounds interesting. Is there a book that tells you how to use them?"

"I'm sure there is, but an easier way is for me to give you a few lessons. Then once you've done some practicing where there's no likelihood of your getting lost, we'll plan a cross country trip, but only after I'm convinced you like backpacking."

"I love it! I want to do it for the rest of my life! I want to get so good at backpacking that I'll be able to go anywhere I want and never get lost. I'm going to be the 21st century's answer to Daniel Boone!"

Mr. Cunningham laughed. "Okay, Daniel, how about you start by getting us to Round Lake."

In a little while, they crossed a creek, and then the trail began to ascend in a series of switchbacks. Afraid Mr. Cunningham might think him too slow, Milton tried to maintain the same pace he held on level ground. Soon he was breathing hard and sweat was dripping down from his face.

"Don't wear yourself out," Mr. Cunningham cautioned. "Backpacking is not a competitive sport. The idea is to enjoy being outdoors, and we've got all day to get to Round Lake."

In a little while, they stopped and drank from their water bottles. "How far do you think we've come?" Milton said.

Mr. Cunningham looked back down the trail. "I'd say about three-quarters of a mile."

"Is that all?"

"Why? Are you getting tired?"

Milton was a little tired, but he wasn't about to admit it. "It just seemed like we'd gone farther. Distances are deceptive when you're hiking on trails."

"Once you've hiked some more, you'll know how to set a pace that's right for you. You don't want to be thinking all the time about how far it is to your destination. You want to be thinking about is how nice it is to be out here."

With that in mind, Milton set a pace that didn't tire himself. But rather than thinking about the forest around him, he found himself thinking about Ramblin' Red. Even though Ramblin' Red was a figment of his imagination, nevertheless Milton wished Ramblin' Red could see him now. In Milton's mind, Ramblin' Red was the ultimate outdoorsman, able to survive with little more than a knife, a gun and a bedroll. Milton's own outdoor experience made him feel more connected to Ramblin' Red than ever before.

"Are we going to sleep out under the stars tonight?" Milton said.

"We'll have to wait and see," Mr. Cunningham said. "Sometimes we get thunderstorms up here in the mountains, so I brought along a tent just in case. But if the weather's good, it would be nice to sleep where we can look up at the stars."

After an hour's more hiking, they stopped along another creek and had a snack of peanuts and raisins. Milton was curious about how far they had come, but didn't want to ask. Mr. Cunningham, however, volunteered the information. "I figure we're about halfway to Round Lake, maybe a little farther. How are you doing? Still feel like the 21st century's answer to Daniel Boone?"

Milton smiled. "I guess backpacking is more work than I'd thought it would be, but it's good work." Milton got up from the rock on which he had been sitting. "It makes me feel like I'm accomplishing something. I mean, it wouldn't be the same if we had driven to Round Lake in a car."

"I think, in time, you'll find hiking will give you more than just a sense of accomplishment. If you're like me, you'll find being outdoors a necessity. It's how I escape the stress of making a living and allows me to reconnect to what's real." He pointed up the trail. "Like that very real black bear there."

Milton spun around to see a large black bear lumbering down the trail toward them. "What should we do?"

Mr. Cunningham pointed. "Let's slowly move off the trail and up that slope."

With heart pounding, Milton went up the slope at a near run. He slipped on the pine-needle-covered ground and slid back down.

With a firm hand, Mr. Cunningham arrested his fall. "I said, 'slowly.' Now, move to the right where it's not so steep. And try to remain calm."

Milton did as instructed, and soon found himself upon a small ridge, looking down upon the trail.

"Okay," Mr. Cunningham said, joining him, "now let's just stand here and wait for the bear to go on by."

Milton felt both frightened and excited. The bear, for its part, seemed unconcerned that there were two humans nearby. It sauntered down the trail, stopping occasionally to sniff at a downed log. When it reached the creek, it stopped for a drink before continuing on down the trail.

Milton waited until the bear was out of sight before speaking. "That was incredible! And it didn't seem to notice us at all."

"Oh, it noticed us, all right. It was just being lazy and using the trail because it's the easiest way to get where it's going. I guess, in that sense, bears are just like us."

"What would've happened if we couldn't have gotten off the trail, or if we had been hiking and came upon the bear all of a sudden and couldn't get out of the way, or if the bear had been behind us and we couldn't see it, or if—"

"That's a whole lot of 'ifs.' Remember the bear doesn't want trouble any more than we do. If the bear had found us blocking the trail, it likely would have gone around us. That said, you should always be respectful of wild animals. I've seen people do stupid things like run after a bear just to see how close they can get to take a picture. When I'm hiking, I try to maintain a relaxed watchfulness, which means I don't want to be constantly on my guard, for that soon gets tiring, but at the same time, I want to be aware of my surroundings so if anything does suddenly show up, like a bear, I won't be taken by surprise. Now let's go back to the creek because I want to show you something."

When they reached the creek, Mr. Cunningham pointed out the bear's footprints at the water's edge. "Study them so that if you ever see them again, you'll know a bear is in the vicinity."

"Those footprints are huge!" Milton exclaimed. "And look, you can see the impression made by its claws."

Mr. Cunningham picked up a stick and used it as a pointer. "Now look right here and here. A bear, when it walks, brings its back foot nearly up to its front."

Milton knelt down and ran his finger along the edge of the footprint where the bear's back foot had sunk deep into the wet ground. "Where the two prints come together it looks like just one big foot print instead of two." His lifted his head. "Hey, Big Foot!"

"That's right," Mr. Cunningham said, smiling. "What some people think is a footprint made by some mysterious creature can easily be explained if you know how a bear walks and the kind of footprint it leaves." Mr. Cunningham tossed the stick aside. "I say we've had quite a day. We've seen both a pileated woodpecker and a black bear."

"Maybe we'll see a mountain lion."

Mr. Cunningham laughed. "Anything's possible."

Following the switchbacks, Milton and Mr. Cunningham climbed higher and higher, and finally reached the top of a ridge where they stopped to rest and to enjoy the view. To the east a tall range of mountains was dusted with snow.

"In a couple of weeks," Mr. Cunningham said, "if it hasn't snowed heavily yet, we'll do a backpacking trip in the high country. It would be easier for me to teach you map and compass technique above the timberline where we'd have a clear view of the peaks."

"Hey, look!" Milton said, pointing. Between the trees, sparkling water could be seen.

"That's Round Lake," Mr. Cunningham said.

"Wow! It's not far at all."

"And it's all downhill from here."

It was past lunchtime by the time they made it to the lake, but Milton was too excited to eat. "Are there any fish in the lake?"

As if to answer his question, a fish leaped out of the water, not twenty feet from shore.

Milton knelt down to feel the water temperature. It was cold, but not too cold. "Can we go swimming?"

"Did you bring your swimming trunks?"

Milton couldn't remember if he had brought them or not. He took off his backpack, leaned it against a tree and began to search through it. "Here they are!" he announced. "Let's go swimming."

"Lunch first. If you're like me, you're hungry enough to eat that bear we saw."

Lunch was crackers and cheese along with dried fruit. They ate, sitting on a granite ledge that stuck out into the lake. From there they could see the whole of the lake. To the east a stand of conifers rose unbroken to a ridge top and beyond the ridge lay the snowy peaks. Milton thought it the most beautiful sight he had ever seen.

"Thank you, Mr. Cunningham. Thanks for taking me backpacking with you."

"Are you having fun?"

"This is the most fun I've had since we moved to Indian Falls."

"I guess Indian Falls is rather a dull sort of place if you're used to the excitement of the city. But, as you can see, it does have its compensations." He started to gather up the remains of lunch. "It'd be a good idea to let your food digest a bit before going swimming. In the meantime, why don't I show you how to use a fly rod?"

Mr. Cunningham gave Milton the task of determining what insects the fish were feeding on while he assembled his fly rod and reel. There were a lot of translucent-winged flies fluttering along the surface of the water. Milton caught one and brought it to Mr. Cunningham.

"That's a mayfly," Mr. Cunningham said. "I'm surprised they're still hatching this late in the year." From a small leather case, he selected a hook disguised to resemble a mayfly. "With all the real mayflies to choose from, the fish most likely won't bite on my imitation, but we'll give it a try anyway."

He demonstrated for Milton how to reel out the line by making repeated casts until there was enough line to fling well out over the water. When Milton tried to do it himself, his line landed in a tangle only a few feet from shore.

"I can see this is going to take a lot of practice," Milton said.

"Next time, I'll bring a spinning reel. It's easier to use."

Milton returned the fly rod to Mr. Cunningham. "If it's okay, I'd like to go swimming."

"Sure. Just don't go off where I can't see you."

After Milton had changed into his swimming trunks, he climbed atop a good jumping rock and stared down into the water. The water was so clear, he could see all the way to the bottom of the lake, a distance he judged to be six to eight feet. Directly below, in the shadow of the rock, several large trout swam in lazy circles.

"Hey, Mr. Cunningham!" Milton yelled. "The fish are over here."

Mr. Cunningham waved, but continued fishing where he was.

"Hey, Mr. Cunningham, watch!" Milton jumped off the rock and in midair curled up into a "cannon ball," a configuration designed to produce the maximum splash. The coldness of the water was a shock. He broke the surface and with teeth chattering looked for the nearest place get out of the water. The jumping rock was too sheer to climb, so he swam toward a sandy beach. Halfway there, he realized he was no longer cold, so he turned on his back and floated, looking up at a cloud drifting overhead. The cloud was a thunderhead, flat on the bottom and billowy on top. As it drifted eastward, it appeared to blow up like a lumpish balloon, pushing higher and higher into the sky. As he continued to float, more clouds appeared, a whole flotilla sailing eastward. Milton imagined himself floating in outer space, looking down at the clouds, the blue sky being the ocean below him.

Suddenly something large struck the water nearby, sending a wave of water over his face. He looked up to see Mr. Cunningham motioning to the west and yelling. Milton shook the water out of his ears to clear them. The first thing he heard was not Mr. Cunningham, but the rumble of thunder rolling in from the east.

"Milton!" Mr. Cunningham cried. "Get out of the lake!"

He swam as fast as he could for the shore. As he waded out of the water, large drops of rain began to pelt him.

"Grab your backpack and follow me!" Mr. Cunningham yelled.

They ran toward a large cedar tree whose sloping branches made a shelter from the rain. The base of the cedar seemed to be a favored spot, for someone had constructed a bench using a plank and two rounds cut from a pine tree. Nearby was a fire pit.

"I hope the lightning doesn't choose to strike this grand old tree," Mr. Cunningham said, leaning his backpack against the tree trunk. "But it's a lot safer here than being in the lake. Water is a great conductor, and you might've been electrocuted had you kept on swimming." As if to emphasize his point, a bolt of lightning lit up the sky, followed by thunder.

After a pause, Milton said, "That lightning strike was about three kilometers away."

"How do you know?"

"Well, practically speaking, we can see a bolt of lightning simultaneously as it strikes, since light travels at approximately 300 million meters per second. Sound, on the other hand, pokes along at the rate of only 343.2 meters per second, or approximately one kilometer every three seconds. I counted nine seconds between seeing the lightning and hearing the thunder, so I knew the lightning struck about three kilometers away."

"That's a neat trick," Mr. Cunningham said. "But I'm of the old school that never really learned the metric system. Can you translate that into miles?"

"Sure. Sound travels at 1,126 feet per second, or approximately one mile every five seconds."

Mr. Cunningham did some quick calculating. "So that last strike was a little less than two miles away."

"Not close enough to have struck the lake."

"Yes, but I wouldn't want to chance it. You never know where lightning might strike."

Milton and Mr. Cunningham sat on the bench and calculated the distances of subsequent lightning strikes. Eventually the edge of the storm moved east to be followed by a gentle rain. Safe and dry under the boughs of the cedar, the two friends sat quietly and watched as raindrops dappled the surface of the lake. After a while, Mr. Cunningham stood and pulled his raingear from his pack.

"What are you doing?" Milton said.

"I've always had better luck fishing in the rain. I think that's because the rain makes it harder for the fish to see my line." He pointed to Milton's pack. "If I were you, I'd change into some dry clothes."

Milton was not that cold, but he did as Mr. Cunningham suggested. Then he sat and watched Mr. Cunningham make repeated casts into the lake. After a while, Mr. Cunningham moved off around the cove and out of sight, leaving Milton alone. Milton did not mind being alone. In fact, one of the few benefits of having moved to the mountains was his discovery that he liked being alone. This seemed to confirm that he was, by nature, a writer, for writing is a lonely pastime. But more than that, a writer needs time alone to create his characters. This was another good thing about backpacking, for its slow pace had given Milton lots of time to think about the story he was writing about Ramblin' Red. But he still did not have any idea why Ramblin Red should lose the contest he was now engaged in.

Chapter 11

Milton poked the foil-wrapped potatoes that earlier had been placed in the ashes of the campfire.

"Are they done yet?" Mr. Cunningham said.

"They're still a little hard, I think," Milton answered.

"Then we'll wait to cook the trout. They won't take but a few minutes once the potatoes are done."

Milton looked at the four plump trout that Mr. Cunningham had caught. The fish had been gutted and cleaned, and only waited for the potatoes to finish baking before being roasted. Milton was so hungry, he could have eaten the fish raw. To confirm this, his stomach grumbled loudly.

Mr. Cunningham laughed. From a bear canister, he took a snack bag with the remains of peanuts and raisins and tossed them to Milton. "There, that ought to hold you."

Two fish suddenly jumped out of the water near to the shore. "They looked like they were playing tag," Milton observed.

"They were probably going after the same mayfly," Mr. Cunningham said.

But seeing one thing seemingly chase after another reminded Milton of the pictures of steer roping he had seen while researching a final contest for Ramblin' Red. "Did you know rodeo competition really didn't get started until the nineteen-thirties?"

"But, if I'm not mistaken, they grew out of competitions held by Mexican *vaqueros* back in the seventeen hundreds."

Milton nodded.

"So, you've decided on a final event in Ramblin' Red's contest?"

"I chose steer roping, because that was something a cowboy had to do." He poked the smallest of the potatoes. "Hey, I think this one's done."

Mr. Cunningham placed the fish atop a wire grill left by a previous camper and set it atop two rocks that straddled the fire. When the fish were done, Mr. Cunningham handed Milton a plate with a large baked potato, drowning in butter, along with a sizzling trout.

"Don't burn your mouth," Mr. Cunningham cautioned.

Milton blew on a flaky piece of trout to cool it then popped it into his mouth. He groaned with pleasure.

"I'll take that to mean it meets with your approval," Mr. Cunningham said.

"This is about the best thing I've ever eaten."

"Well, you can't beat fresh trout, only watch for bones."

The two friends ate in companionable silence. When they were done, they wrapped the remains of their dinner in foil and placed them in one of the bear canisters. Then they nibbled on cookies and watched as the first stars appeared in the sky.

"I bet you know just about everybody in Indian Falls," Milton said.

"I wouldn't say everybody, but Indian Falls is a small place, and except for a short stint in the Army, I've lived there my whole life."

"Do you know Karl Kastorsky?"

"What makes you ask about ol' Karl?"

Milton explained about his encounter with Karl Kastorsky at the market and his being pushed down onto the hard concrete.

"That sounds about like Karl," Mr. Cunningham said in response. "Still, you shouldn't have been trying to get up on his trailer. Folks get a mite protective of that which provides their livelihood, and you can't blame them."

"But he didn't even give me a chance to explain before he shoved me."

"I'm not about to defend what he did, but Karl's gone though some hard times, and I guess that's made him a bit short-tempered."

"I heard his wife died."

"Which happened right after he lost his job when the mill closed, leaving him with a mountain of medical bills and no money to pay for them."

"Couldn't he have gone to work at the new mill?"

"And leave the mountains? He'd rather die first."

Mr. Cunningham gathered up the plates and utensils. "I guess these won't wash themselves."

Milton jumped up. "Let me wash them."

"All right." Mr. Cunningham handed Milton a small pan. "Fill that with water then rinse off the plates over there." He pointed to a patch of ground in front of a nearby bush. "If you need to, use a little sand as a scouring powder. Then toss the dirty water on that bush. That way we'll keep the lake clean and concentrate all the food smells in this one area."

While Milton washed dishes, Mr. Cunningham placed the bear canisters well away from where they had been eating. By the time they were both done, it was nearly dark. They returned to the campfire, which had burned down to coals.

"Are you cold?" Mr. Cunningham said.

Milton was wearing the sweater he had brought. "Not really."

"Then I won't put any more wood on the fire. That way we'll be able to see the stars better. Have you ever seen so many?"

Milton never had. "We studied the constellations in the last school I went to, only they look a lot different in real life than in photos." He pointed to a cloud of stars arching across the sky. "I know that's the Milky Way, and that group of stars over there that looks like a big "W" is Cassiopeia." He pointed to the left of Cassiopeia. "That, of course, is the Big Dipper."

"Can you find Polaris, which is also called the North Star?"

"Which way is north?"

"North is in the direction of the Big Dipper."

"Then is it that bright star there?"

"No, that's Arcturus. To find the North Star, start at the handle of the Dipper and go all the way out to the other end. The last two stars point directly at it."

"I see it!" Milton exclaimed.

"The North Star is always in the same place in the sky, so if you're ever lost, orient yourself to where you're facing it. Then you'll know that east is to your right and west to your left."

"What if it's cloudy?"

"In that case you better hope you brought along a compass." He yawned. "All this exercise and clear mountain air has made me sleepy. I think I'll turn in."

"Is it okay if I stay up a little longer?"

"Sure, only let's set out our sleeping bags first."

Mr. Cunningham chose a spot for them to sleep that was well away from the campfire, where the smells from their meal might attract a bear. He then used a foot pump to inflate two air mattresses. "Of course, if we were true mountain men we would've cut conifer branches to use as bedding."

"I think even mountain men would have found air mattresses beat pokey pine needles," Milton said.

"I admit there are some advantages to modern living. Did you bring your flashlight?"

Milton took out his flashlight and flicked it on and off.

"Then enjoy looking at the stars. If I weren't so tired I'd stay up and watch them with you. The moon will be rising in about an hour."

Milton followed the trail that led to the jumping rock. There he had an unobstructed view of the sky. The dark sky provided a velvety backdrop for the jewel-like stars. The mountains appeared darker still. He theorized that, black as the sky was, it was still illuminated by the light of the stars, whereas the peaks had no light of their own.

Or so he thought. Near to the craggy top of the highest peak, known as

Broken Arrow, a light suddenly appeared and just as suddenly was gone. Milton thought his eyes were playing tricks on him until he saw the light again, faintly at first then brighter before disappearing again.

Milton realized there was someone up there. But what could he be doing way up there at this time of night? Was he lost? Was he in trouble? Milton thought he should wake Mr. Cunningham.

He hurried back along the trail. "Mr. Cunningham, are you awake?"

Mr. Cunningham turned over in his sleeping bag. "What is it, Milton?"

"There's a strange light I think you should see."

Mr. Cunningham rolled out of his sleeping bag and quickly slipped into his hiking boots. "Show me."

Milton led the way back to the jumping rock. "You can't see it now, but I saw it just a minute ago up there." He pointed to Broken Arrow.

"It's probably a light from—"

"There! Do you see it?"

"I do indeed. It's just as I thought, a rock climber has made a bivouac and is using his flashlight to either cook dinner or set up his sleeping hammock."

"What's a bivouac?"

"It's a camp, only unlike ours, the rock climber is having to make his on the vertical face of Broken Arrow."

"Is he okay?"

"Oh, sure. Broken Arrow is popular with rock climbers, and it usually takes climbers two days to climb it. I'm just surprised that whoever is up there chose to climb it so late in the season. Come the morning, that granite face will be slick with frost."

"Now the light's gone away."

Mr. Cunningham tapped Milton on the shoulder. "Let me see your flashlight."

Milton handed it to him.

"I got a hunch I know who's crazy enough to be up there." Directing the beam of the flashlight at Broken Arrow, Mr. Cunningham intermittently covered the lens with his hand.

"What are you doing?"

"I'm sending Morse code to whoever's up there."

"What are you saying?"

"I'm asking if that person is Karl Kastorsky?"

Soon the light on Broken Arrow was answering back. "Wow! What's he saying?" Milton said.

"He's asking if I'm Jim Cunningham." Mr. Cunningham answered in the affirmative.

"Now what's he saying?"

Mr. Cunningham laughed. "He's calling me a bunch of names. Most of them unrepeatable."

That sounds like Karl Kastorsky, Milton thought.

"I'm now telling him that I'm camping here at Round Lake with a friend."

When the signal came back, Mr. Cunningham laughed again. "He's saying it's past bedtime for an old fart like me."

"He should talk!"

Mr. Cunningham signaled back. "I'm telling him what you just said."

"Don't let him know it's me!"

In a few seconds the signal was answered.

"What did he say?"

Mr. Cunningham chuckled. "You don't want to know." He quickly signaled a response then turned the flashlight off and handed it back to Milton. "Well, that was fun."

"Where did you learn Morse code?"

"In Eagle Scouts. In fact, Karl and I learned together." Mr. Cunningham pointed over Milton's shoulder. "Milton, look!"

A gibbous moon had risen above the horizon, its light casting a silver path across the lake to where they stood. Of all the wonders Milton had seen that day–the pileated woodpecker, the bear, the thunder storm, the light shining out from Broken Arrow–the sparkling moon path was the most magical. "Doesn't it look like you could just walk right out on it?"

"I'd suggest putting back on your swimming trunks first." Mr. Cunningham stretched out his arms and yawned. "Are you sleepy yet?"

"A little. But I'd like to stay up a bit longer."

Milton was more tired than he let on, but he had some thinking he wanted to do. As he sat admiring the moon path, it came to him the reason why Ramblin' Red should lose the contest.

Chapter 12

The mayor of Pandemonium looked out over the crowd gathered beside the corral behind the livery stable. Reaching into the pocket of his coat, he took out a slip of paper.

"Gentlemen, this is how things stand. Nero Marceau, who has elected to sit out the final event, has the lead with ten points. Second place is a tie between Randy Stark and Ramblin' Red, each with seven points." The mayor read off names of the other contenders. None had sufficient points to claim the prize money even if he were to win the final event.

"Now, this last contest was something Shorty and me thought up ourselves," the mayor continued.

"That's right," Shorty chimed in. "We figured since most of you have spent some time around a cow, one end or the other, you all should know how to lasso one if need be."

"As soon as the steer breaks out of the holding pen," the mayor said, "the clock will start. Each contestant will then see how fast he can rope the steer, bring it to ground, and tie its feet–just like you were preparing to brand it. The man with the fastest time will be declared the winner."

The first contestant was Buck, the cowboy who had fallen off his horse during the horse race. Buck sat easy on his mustang, lightly resting his lariat on his thigh as he waited for an uncooperative steer to be pushed into the holding pen. But as soon as the steer was released, Buck and the mustang shot out after it. The steer had barely got up to running speed before Buck had it lassoed. Then as the mustang kept tension upon the rope, Buck, nimble as a dancer, leaped from the saddle, wrestled the steer to the ground and tied its feet.

"Eight seconds!" the mayor announced.

The crowd went wild, cheering, stomping, slapping each other on the back as if they themselves had executed Buck's amazing feat. In response to this ovation, Buck removed his hat and bowed low.

Ramblin' Red, who had been leaning on the rail as he watched Buck's performance, shook his head. "I have about as much chance of beating that time as I would getting milk out of a bull."

Sheriff Roswell, standing beside him, nodded in agreement. "But just think how fast Buck would've been had he been sober."

Ramblin' Red wasn't the only one who didn't stand a chance of beating Buck, but that still did not discourage other contestants from trying, if for no other reason than the sheer fun of it. Among those who managed to rope a steer, none was able to tie it up in less than a minute.

When it came Ramblin' Red's turn, he was determined to make a good show. He gave Cricket an encouraging pat. "Okay, Cricket, we've done this a thousand times. Just do your job, and I'll do mine." Ramblin' Red did not have to best Buck's time, but only to do better than Randy Stark in order to claim the one hundred dollars in prize money and the extra two hundred Nero Marceau had contributed. He looked across the stockyard where Stark stood, surrounded by four scrawny boys. That look cost Ramblin' Red a precious second, for the steer was released as Ramblin' Red sat staring. Yet once started, everything went like clockwork. With a flip of his wrist, he flung his lariat out over the horns of the steer then wrapped the other end around the horn of his saddle. Even before Cricket had pulled the rope taut, Ramblin' Red was out of his saddle, racing toward the steer. The steer proved more obstinant than Buck's and Ramblin' Red had to dig his boot heels hard into the dirt before he was able to pitch the steer onto its side. Then it was but an instant before he had its legs tied.

"Twelve seconds!" the mayor announced.

Again, the crowd erupted with cheering. In response, Ramblin' Red doffed his hat as he led Cricket from the corral.

Sheriff Roswell met him with a congratulatory handshake. "If you had gotten a little quicker start, I do believe you would've equaled Buck's time."

Ramblin' Red patted Cricket's neck. "It's a good thing one of us wasn't sleeping."

"I reckon that prize money is as good as yours." The sheriff looked across the stockyard where Randy Stark was preparing to mount his horse. "Which is just as well."

Ramblin' Red turned to face the sheriff. "Why? What do you know about Stark?"

"He's a nester, horning in on a patch of land about three miles out of town—just him and those four brats of his."

"No wife?"

"She died of consumption last winter." The sheriff shook his head. "When are these no-good nesters going to learn that this ain't farm land? It's range land. Always was, always will be."

Ramblin' Red understood Sheriff Roswell's aversion to nesters. It was an attitude he more or less shared. More and more homesteaders were moving in, fencing off the range land, making it harder and harder to move cattle around to graze. That said, being a nester didn't necessarily make someone a villain.

Ramblin' Red and the sheriff watched as Randy Stark waited for his steer to be released from the holding pen.

"He's forgot his lariat," the sheriff said.

The sheriff was right. As Stark sat poised to go after his steer, his hands held nothing but the reins of his horse.

Ramblin' Red scratched his head. "What the—"

Further comment was cut off by the steer exploding out of the holding pen. Stark and his horse were after it in a flash. The horse brought Stark right alongside the steer and Stark sprang from his saddle, landed on the steer and grabbed it about the neck. Stark's boot heels plowed two furrows in the dirt as he braked the steer to a halt. Then twisting the steer's neck, he flipped it on its side and quickly tied its feet together.

The crowd was stunned into silence. No one had ever seen a man wrestle a steer bare handed. During that silence, the mayor checked his stop watch then checked it again. "Twelve seconds!" he announced.

"Wait a minute!" Lucky Lars Skogland yelled. He pointed to Stark, who was dusting off his clothes. "He can't do that!" Lucky looked around. "Can he?"

Thereupon an argument broke out as to whether Stark's manner of steer-roping–if it could be called that since the contestant did not use a rope–should be allowed. Ramblin' Red did not follow the debate, but instead pondered what would make a man risk life and limb jumping onto the back of a steer? If the steer had turned its head at the wrong moment, Stark would have been impaled on its horns. The gruesome image of a steer's horn protruding from Stark's back played over and over again in his mind. He shook his head to clear it then found everyone staring at him.

"So what's it to be, Ramblin' Red?" the mayor said.

"Sorry, mayor, I haven't been paying attention."

"We all decided that since you've got the most at stake in this contest, you should decide whether Stark should be disqualified or not."

"He should be!" Lucky Lars Skogland shouted.

It was little wonder that Lucky would be set against Stark, for Lucky was a rancher with little love for nesters. But just because Stark was a nester it did not make it right that he should be disqualified. Then again, was it right for Stark to have yanked Ramblin' Red's foot out of the stirrup during the horse race? Now Ramblin' Red's had opportunity to get back at Stark.

Ramblin' Red looked up into the sky where the rosy clouds were reflecting the sun's fading light. Yes, Ramblin' Red wanted to settle matters with Stark, but not like this; not with some cheap, lawyer's trick. When the time came to deal with Stark he would do so man to man, face to face.

Ramblin' Red turned to the mayor. "Stark got the job done. In my way of thinking, that's all that counts."

"In that case," the mayor said, "there'll have to be a run-off." He burrowed his hand down into the pocket of his pants and came out with a silver dollar. "I'm going to flip a coin. If it comes up heads, Ramblin' Red will go first; tails, Stark goes first." Everyone watched as the coin, spinning high in the air, caught the slanting rays of sunlight. It landed on the ground tail side up.

"Okay, gentleman," the mayor said, "it'll be dark soon, so let's get this contest over with so we can all go enjoy some refreshment."

As Stark rode his horse into the corral, Ramblin' Red thought again about what would make a man risk his life by jumping on top of a steer. He looked across the corral where Stark's four boys sat atop the railing. They appeared to range in age from around seven to perhaps fourteen. Rather than frisking about and showing the excitement one would expect, they sat, looking like four pint-sized undertakers. Ramblin' Red saw that none of the boys wore shoes and the jeans each was wearing had holes in them. And just seeing how emaciated each boy looked made his own stomach grumble as if he had not eaten in days.

The holding pen opened and Stark and his horse shot out after the steer. Though Stark was as quick to leap upon the steer, he had a harder time getting it stopped. Then it was all he could do to wrestle the steer to the ground. By the time he tied its feet, he was reeling from exhaustion.

The mayor looked at his stop watch. "Thirty-seven seconds!"

Sheriff Roswell slapped Ramblin' Red on the back. "That three hundred dollars is as good as yours."

Three hundred dollars! With that kind of money Ramblin' Red could ramble for years without needing to hire on with some rancher. He had always wanted to ramble on down to Mexico. He pictured himself dancing beneath the stars with a dark-eyed *señorita*.

Then his stomach grumbled again.

This time he and Cricket lost no time getting after the steer. In fact, Cricket leaped forward with such speed, he bumped against the steer and had to slow in order to give Ramblin' Red space to swing his lariat. Ramblin' Red's twirling lariat creating a loop like a giant halo above himself and Cricket. But just as he was prepared to make his throw, something came over him. He had tossed the lariat so many times he could do it without thinking. This time, however, his hand seemed to have a will of its own, and at the last second, jerked back, causing the loop to close too soon. It fell over one horn of the steer then slipped off. By the time Ramblin' Red had re-coiled his lariat to try again, it was already too late.

From the far side of the corral came cheers as four, now jubilant, boys leaped from the railing and clambered all over their father. Ramblin' Red, for his part, just leaned back in the saddle and stared up into the sky. A sprinkling of stars in the azure heavens made for a pretty sight. But all Ramblin' Red imagined seeing were three hundred, one-dollar bills being carried away by the wind.

Chapter 13

Milton was bored. Bored to the point of wanting to scream. Bored enough to want to hurl tomatoes at Miss Droshky who was droning on about quadratic equations.

Milton did not know why tomatoes. He did not have any tomatoes. But the thought of an overly ripe tomato plastered to Miss Droshky's head and sticky tomato juice dribbling down her collar was a palliative to his suffering.

The problem was he had gotten out his writing pad only to have Miss Droshky confiscate it again. When Milton had tried to reason that he was not planning to write in it, but only reread what he had written, Miss Droshky had responded by giving him another detention. Now Milton could look forward to being bored during lunch as well.

He looked about the room. The other students looked bored too. He thought the problem had less to do with the subject than the way it was being taught, for Miss Droshky looked as bored as her students; bored and a little menacing, as if to say, "sure I know I'm boring, but what are you going to do about it?"

Milton wished he knew what he could do about it. But short of running out the door, which would earn him a week of detentions, he couldn't think of anything.

"Lots of times," Miss Droshky intoned, "you are going to come across a quadratic equation that's not easy to factor. In that case, you can use the quadratic formula, which is..." She turned to write on the chalkboard, "... x is equal to minus b, plus or minus the square root of b squared, minus $4ac$, all over $2a$." She turned back to the class. "Now, this formula is your friend, so you'll want to memorize it."

"Yeah, right," Rudy Kastorsky muttered.

"I heard that, Rudy," Miss Droshky said. "If you're going to get anywhere in mathematics—and judging from your last test score, you're not—then you're going to have to memorize formulas far more difficult than this."

"But why memorize when you just can look them up?"

"Why use your brain at all, Rudy? Why not just sit around watching TV and eating donuts all day?"

Rudy stared down at his desk. "Sounds good to me," he muttered.

Miss Droshky turned to acknowledge Milton's raised hand. "What is it, Milton?"

"We could devise a mnemonic," he said.

"That's a nice word, Milton, but I'm not sure all your classmates know what it means."

Katie spoke up. "A mnemonic is an aid to memory, like if you can't remember how many days in a month, you say, "thirty days has September, April—"

"Thank you Katie," Miss Droshky said, holding her chalk out like it was the handle of a sword. "But people who learn to use their brains don't have to rely on silly gimmicks."

"But what's wrong with a mnemonic if it makes learning easier?" Milton said.

"Fine, Milton, if you want to figure out some mnemonic to help you memorize the quadratic formula, go right ahead. But do it on your own time instead of wasting ours."

Mark De Angelo, a student with a talent for music raised his hand.

Miss Droshky let out a weary sigh. "Yes, Mark, what is it?"

" 'Pop Goes the Weasel.' "

"What?"

"The quadratic formula fits the tune 'Pop Goes the Weasel.' "

Now the class looked interested.

"How?" someone said.

"Sing it for us, Mark," Katie said.

Miss Droshky dropped her chalk onto her desk. "Yes, sing it for us. After all, I'm just the teacher. Why listen to me?"

As Miss Droshky slumped down in her desk chair, Mark De Angelo stood up.

"Okay, it goes like this." And he began to sing.

"*x* is equal to minus *b*
plus or minus the square root
of *b* squared minus 4*ac*
all over 2*a*."

"Very clever, Mark," Miss Droshky said, rising to her feet, "but now–"

Brenda Miller was frantically waving her arm.

"Now what?" Miss Droshky said.

Like Rudy, Brenda had difficulties with math. "Please, Miss Droshky, it would really help me remember the formula if we could practice Mark's song a few times together."

Before Miss Droshky could object, Mark tapped his pencil on his desk as if it were a conductor's baton. "Miss Droshky's sixth grade algebra class will now perform the quadratic formula to the tune of 'Pop Goes the Weasel.' Ready?"

"Wait a second," Juan Ortiz said, as he quickly opened his clarinet case and began to assemble the parts.

"Let me get out my flute!" Jennifer Geisler exclaimed.

When Juan and Jennifer finished tuning, Mark waved his pencil again. "Okay. One and two and…" Their performance, though enthusiastic, was fairly ragged, so Mark commanded the class to sing it again. "And this time everybody stand up."

The second time around was much better. The third time they added a clap on the word 'all' where "pop" would have been. The fourth time they added a stomp. The fifth time, Mrs. Reese, the principal, walked in.

"What's all this?"

"We're singing a song to help us memorize the quadratic formula," Milton said.

Mrs. Reese looked at Miss Droshky. "This I want to hear."

The class sang out as Mrs. Reese tapped her foot in time to the music.

"Very good," Mrs. Reese said. "But does your song really work?" She went to the chalkboard and erased the quadratic formula that Miss Droshky had written. Turning, she held out the chalk to Brenda, whose difficulties in math were familiar to Mrs. Reese. "Okay, Brenda, see if you can now write out the quadratic formula from memory."

Brenda hummed along as she correctly wrote the formula on the board. As she set the chalk down her classmates, along with Mrs. Reese, applauded her performance.

Mrs. Reese turned to Miss Droshky, "I'd call that very creative teaching, Miss Droshky. Keep up the good work!"

Miss Droshky, who bore the look of someone lost in a maze, managed to mumble a thank you. After Mrs. Reese left, Miss Droshky instructed the class to spend the remainder of the period reading the next chapter. Then she hid herself behind a large travel brochure, which she did not emerge from even when the bell rang, ending class.

"What's her problem?" Katie whispered to Milton as she gathered up her books.

Milton shook his head.

"Watch yourself," Katie warned.

Even with the class emptied of students, Miss Droshky remained walled behind her travel brochure. With boredom seeping back in, Milton looked about for something of interest. He noticed that Rudy had left a paperback on his desk that looked to be science fiction. Milton was not interested in science fiction. What *did* interest him was the illustration on the book cover. It showed a herd of wild beasts that looked like giant warthogs bearing down upon a man in a spacesuit wielding a sword. It was the expression on the man's face that intrigued Milton, for the man looked back at the reader with a big smile on his face, as if the prospect of being trampled by a herd of giant warthogs was the greatest thing on earth. It was an expression Ramblin' Red might have exhibited, faced with one of his perilous adventures.

"I suppose you think you're smarter than I am."

Milton spun about to see Miss Droshky staring out over the top of her brochure. Not knowing how to respond, Milton stalled for time. "Are you planning a vacation, Miss Droshky?"

"Don't change the subject. Answer the question."

He thought the question unfair, designed to get him in more hot water no matter how he answered. But upon reflection, he *did* think himself smarter than Miss Droshky, which was not to say he possessed Miss Droshky's knowledge, for she had more years of learning behind her. Yet if making a comparison of basic intelligence, Milton believed himself smarter. But he was not about to say that.

"You're smarter, Miss Droshky. After all, that's why you're the teacher."

"Don't try to butter me up! One look at your face tells me you think you're smarter. Well, let me tell you something, Mr. Smarty Pants, I'm not going to always be wasting my life, teaching a bunch of pimply adolescents how to think. I've got plans. One of these days I'm going to set sail to places you can only dream of going to."

Milton thought that day couldn't come too soon. "I'm glad for you, Miss Droshky."

Miss Droshky snorted, then once again buried herself behind her brochure.

"Excuse me, Miss Droshky, may I read?"

Miss Droshky spoke from behind a picture of a sailboat drifting through turquoise water. "Is it something other than your scribbles?"

"Uh… it's science."

"In that case, go ahead."

Milton reached over and grabbed Rudy's paperback. Being science fiction, Milton was convinced he was not going to like it, but after reading just a few pages, he was hooked, and it was with great reluctance that he returned it to Rudy's desk once the lunch period ended.

But not before writing down the book's author and title: Harry Harrison. *The Stainless Steel Rat Sings the Blues.* What a great title!

Chapter 14

The cabin Milton's grandfather had built was not large, for it was meant to be a vacation home, not a permanent residence. Yet it was big enough for Milton and his grandmother. The two-story cabin had a steeply pitched roof to shed snow. Downstairs was a living room with a dining table at one end, though they usually ate their meals at the counter that separated the kitchen from where they hung their coats near the back door. Upstairs were two bedrooms separated by a bathroom. Because of the steepness of the roof, each bedroom had no side walls, but a ceiling that started at a peak seven feet above Milton's head and slanted down in opposite directions to the edges of the floor. This made Milton's bedroom seem like a huge tent, a rustic feel reinforced by Milton's steel bed frame and the unfinished wood flooring.

Opposite the bedroom door was the room's only window, and beneath that window Milton sat at his desk, writing, or rather, trying to write. Now that Ramblin' Red had lost the contest, Milton did not know the direction his story should take, and Walt was not offering any suggestions. That he had hit upon a dry spell in his writing didn't trouble Milton, for he knew that such spells were common to writers. When after a quarter of an hour he still had not come up with any ideas, he decided instead to work on the theme of the writing contest: "Why do I write?" Unlike when writing fiction, no images came to mind. Perhaps that was because there was nothing to imagine; writing an essay is the not the same as telling a story, but rather establishing a logical sequence of related ideas.

Or was it? Perhaps an essayist sees ideas as if they were characters in a story, as vivid in the essayist's mind as Ramblin' Red was in Milton's. With that in mind, Milton took up his pencil.

I am Milton Mickelsen. I am twelve years old, and I live a very lonely life.

Milton went on to describe his life in Indian Falls and how writing made up for the lack of social opportunities. Yet as he wrote, a disturbing feeling crept over him, one that came whenever he wrote something that lacked the note of truth. When he had lived in the city, he had never lacked for friends, yet that had not kept him from writing. In fact, having friends only increased his desire to write, for he had always looked forward to sharing his efforts with other members of his school's writing club.

With a sigh, Milton set his pencil down. He didn't know why he wrote, he just did. He picked up the sci-fi novel he had checked out of the school library. He discovered that the Stainless Steel Rat was the main character in a series of novels. Unable to get the same book Rudy had been reading, he checked out *The Stainless Steel Rat for President* instead. As he sat reading, he became so engrossed in the story, he failed to hear the knock at the front door.

From the bottom of the stairs, Marta called up to him. "Milton, Mr. Cunningham is here to see you."

Milton went racing down the stairs.

"I thought if you're not busy," Mr. Cunningham said, "we might get started using a map and compass."

"Great!" Milton went to get his jacket.

"Goodness, Jim!" Marta said. "You didn't drive out all this way just for that?"

"Might as well teach Milton while he still shows an interest."

Milton returned with his jacket. "Let's go!"

"Whoa there, partner. We've got some classroom learning to do first." He pointed to the dining table. "Is it okay to spread my things out here?"

"You go right ahead," Marta said, "and while you two navigators are busy,

I'll work on dinner."

Mr. Cunningham opened a large map. "This is what's called a topographical map, or topo map for short. It happens to be a map of this area."

"Cool!" Milton said.

Mr. Cunningham explained the map's symbols and how to read the topography lines. "Not all topo maps are alike. It depends upon how big an area the map is covering. Consequently, the distances in elevations between topo lines may vary. You can get the distances by looking at the map's legend, but I find it just as easy to look at the darker topo lines, which have the elevation written on them, then count number of the lightly drawn lines between them."

Milton counted four lines between two elevations that differed by one thousand feet. "Each topo line indicates an elevation difference of two hundred feet."

"Right. So, what does it mean when the lines are all bunched up together?"

"It means that area is really steep."

"And when they're far apart?"

"The area is pretty flat."

"Good. Now, let me show you how to use the compass with the map. First off, you've got to realize that the compass reads magnetic north, which is different from true north." He explained about degrees of declination and how to adjust the compass to account for the difference between the two "norths." "Now see if you can find where your cabin is located on the map."

"That's easy," Milton said, tracing his finger along the highway shown on the map. "We're right here before the big bend."

"Actually that tiny square on the map is your cabin."

"Really?"

"Yes. A lot of these detailed maps show buildings. Now, let's suppose you wanted to walk from your cabin to Broken Arrow." Mr. Cunningham took a ruler and used it to align the two points. "Now watch. I'll set the compass against the edge of the ruler. We want that little red arrow on the plate outside the compass to be pointed in the direction we want to go, toward Broken Arrow. Now, I want you to rotate the bezel of the compass so that those lines you see on the compass align with the lines on the map."

"Shouldn't we turn the map so it's oriented toward the north?"

"That's good thinking, but right now we're just trying to find the direction to Broken Arrow in degrees. By the way, those lines on map are called latitude and longitude lines."

"Okay, I think I have the lines on the compass aligned with those."

"That looks good. So, if we're going to walk to Broken Arrow from your house, what direction will we go?"

Milton studied the compass. "The pointer says thirty-six degrees north-northwest."

Mr. Cunningham smiled. "I see you're going to pick this up quick."

"Is that it?"

"No, now we've got to apply what you just learned to the field. Grab your jacket."

Marta stuck her head out of the kitchen doorway. "Dinner will be in about ten minutes. You'll be staying for dinner won't you, Jim?" She made this sound more like a command than a question.

"Thanks, Marta, I'd like that."

"Here's a most important point I want you to remember," Mr. Cunningham said, once he and Milton were outside. "Notice the needle on the compass has one side that's red and the other black. You always want the red side pointed toward the north. Don't ask me the number of times I've not done that and wound up going in the exact opposite direction I wanted to go. Now, is the compass still set at thirty-six degrees north-northwest?"

"It is."

"Okay, now hold the compass level and rotate the whole thing until the red end of the needle is inside the outline of the needle painted on the back plate. This is called 'putting Red in the shed.'"

"Okay, Red's in the shed."

"Now, see that other red arrow on the plate outside the compass?"

"Yes."

"That's the direction of Broken Arrow."

"Wow! So, if I walked that way, I'd run into Broken Arrow."

"Theoretically, yes."

"What do you mean?"

"I mean, you can't see Broken Arrow from here. So, in order to get to it, using a compass, you have to navigate point-to-point."

"Show me!"

Mr. Cunningham laughed. "That'll have to wait for another time. We don't want to be late for that good dinner I'm smelling."

Milton hardly said a word during dinner, for he was thinking about what Mr. Cunningham had taught him. After dinner, while Mr. Cunningham and Marta talked over old times, Milton returned to the dining table and practiced his map and compass skills. Everyone was enjoying themselves so much, no one noticed how late it was getting. Finally, Mr. Cunningham stood up to go.

"Goodness!" Marta said. "Where'd the time go? It's way past Milton's bedtime."

"It's my fault," Mr. Cunningham said. "I spend so much time by myself, when I have the pleasure of someone's company, I just can't seem to stop yapping."

"I'm just as bad, Jim."

"Mr. Cunningham," Milton interrupted, "I figured out what you mean by navigating point-to-point."

"So soon?"

Milton nodded. "If you can't see the place you're trying to get to, then you navigate to the farthest point you *can* see. And from there you navigate to the next point you can see, and you keep on navigating point-to-point until you finally get to the place you're trying to get to."

Mr. Cunningham picked up his compass. "I see I'm going to have to get you a better compass than this one, if you're going to be out there in the woods, finding your way around."

"But Jim," Marta said, "is it safe for Milton to be out there on his own?"

"Marta, I trust Milton. In fact, if I was ever lost or injured in the woods, I'd trust Milton to find help."

Mr. Cunningham's comment made Milton feel proud while at the same time a little scared. Could he really find his way through the forest with just a compass and a map? And if it came to it, could he use his skill to save someone's life?

Chapter 15

"Class, before we get started, there's something I wish to show you." Miss Droshky held up a flyer. "I received this in my mailbox yesterday. Now, how many of you have been to the Exploratorium in Bayside?"

Several hands went up.

"Well, the Exploratorium is hosting a science fair in December, and it's open to all middle school students. Is there anyone here who thinks he'd like to participate?"

A few hands went up, then a few more. Eight, all total.

"That's more than I thought there'd be. There's a problem, however. As you know, there have been cutbacks in school funding, but I talked to Mrs. Reese, and she says there's money enough to send a vanload of participants to the fair."

Brenda Miller raised her hand. "But what if more people want to go?"

"Yeah," Juan Ortiz said. "A van hardly holds more than eight people."

"Actually, Juan, there'll only be room for six," Miss Droshky said. "We also have to have room for the science projects."

"So, who gets to go?" Milton said.

"If all of you will be quiet for a minute, I'll tell you. Mrs. Reese and I have decided to hold our own science fair right here at McKinley. We shall have a panel of judges, and the top two winners from each grade will represent us at the Exploratorium. Because the deadline for entries at the Exploratorium is October 31st, we'll be holding our science fair on the evening of the 22nd. That only gives you a month to prepare."

Milton raised his hand.

"Milton, you're always full of questions."

"I just wanted to know if we can enter as a team?"

"Yes, but for obvious reasons your team will have to be limited to two persons, unless, of course, you can get someone from another grade to go in with you. Now, that's all I'm going to say about this right now. Anyone interested can pick up a copy of the entry form after class. I think you'll find it has all the information you need to know. Now, please get out your books and open them to page seventy-three."

While people were getting out their books, Milton turned to Katie. "Do you want to work with me on the science fair?" he whispered.

"Do you have any ideas?"

"I've got a great one."

"Milton!" Miss Droshky yelled. "Where's your book?"

"Okay," Katie said, as Milton took his seat beside her on the bus, "what's your great science idea."

"The science of navigation."

"How did you come up with that one?"

Milton explained how Mr. Cunningham had been teaching him map and compass skills. "It's really fun, and there's a lot to it. I mean we could start with the very first explorers and go all the way up to the current use of global positioning satellites."

"I like history, so I'd enjoy working on that aspect."

"Great!"

"But I don't know anything about using a compass."

"I'll show you. I've been thinking about going out in the forest and doing some point-to-point navigation. What are you doing Saturday?"

Katie smiled. "I guess I'm learning to use a map and compass. I just hope you won't get us lost."

"I won't. But if it'll make you feel any better, I'm going to discuss my plans with Mr. Cunningham."

When Mr. Cunningham arrived at Milton's stop, Milton was ready with the topo map that Mr. Cunningham had left with him. "Can I show you something?"

"Sure," Mr. Cunningham said, turning off the bus engine.

Milton opened the map and laid it out on the seat across the aisle. "I told Katie we'd do some point-to-point navigation on Saturday."

"Why Katie?"

Milton explained about their science project.

"That's a terrific idea. I'll look forward to seeing what you two come up with."

"I was just wondering what you thought of this idea for practicing point-to-point navigation." He pointed to a small circle of topo lines labeled "Slick Rock" on the map. "I've seen this dome lots of times from the highway. It's almost in a straight line between our cabin and Broken Arrow, which we ought to be able to see from the top of the dome."

Mr. Cunningham nodded. "By getting to Slick Rock, you can also confirm if the trajectory we plotted the other night is correct."

"Right. And I think there's little chance of us getting lost. The highway circles Slick Rock halfway around, so if we *did* get lost, we could just go east to the highway."

"And it looks like you'll also be crossing three streambeds, any of which you could follow down to the highway. There's just one problem."

"What's that?"

"The compass you've been using, I doubt is accurate enough for what you want to do."

Milton looked disappointed.

"But this one is," Mr. Cunningham said, pulling a compass from the pocket of his jacket. "It has a mirror which allows you to see the face of the compass as you look through the sight. That way you can get a really accurate reading."

"Wow!" Milton said, holding the compass and looking through the sight. "Can I borrow this for Saturday?"

"It's yours to keep."

Milton lowered the compass. "It must be awfully expensive. I'm not sure I can pay you back."

"You can pay me by winning the science fair. Also by entertaining me with some more adventures of Ramblin' Red. By the way, how's he doing?"

"Not so good. I'm kind of stuck." He explained about Ramblin' Red losing the contest and his reason. "I've kind of run out of ideas about where the story will go next. I've introduced a few characters—there's Nero Marceau, Randy Stark and the lady in lavender—I'm just not sure how they'll all fit in."

Mr. Cunningham closed his eyes and thought for a moment. "Maybe what you need is a 'love interest.'"

"I thought of that. I just don't want my story to get all mushy." Milton thought of Miss Droshky and her romance novels.

"Mushy? It doesn't have to be mushy. Think of Boone Caudill and Teal Eye in *The Big Sky*. That's not mushy. That's tragedy. It's the western version of *Othello*."

Milton smiled. "Okay, I'll think about it."

"And I'd better think about getting back to the bus barn."

As Mr. Cunningham folded up the map, Milton retrieved his backpack. "Thanks a lot for the compass, Mr. Cunningham."

Mr. Cunningham handed Milton the map. "And keep this, too. You'll certainly be needing it come Saturday. Just don't make me have to send Search and Rescue out after you."

"I won't."

Mr. Cunningham opened the bus door. "Keep your powder dry, partner."

"Watch your topknot, and I'll watch mine."

Chapter 16

Marta finished wrapping sandwiches then placed them inside Milton's backpack. "I still don't think this is such a good idea."

"I don't know either," said Mrs. Larsen, Katie's mother, who leaned against Marta's kitchen counter and watched as Milton and Katie prepared to leave.

"You ought to trust Milton, Mom," Katie said.

"I *do* trust Milton. I think he's a very capable boy. But a lot of things could go wrong out there in the woods."

"I've discussed our plans with Mr. Cunningham," Milton said. "And if anything should go wrong, we can always get back to the highway."

"That's if you're able to."

"Please, Mother," Katie said, "nothing will happen. It's a beautiful day with not a cloud in the sky. And if we don't do this, we won't be able to enter the science fair."

Mrs. Larsen still did not look happy. "I see I'm going to be doing nothing but worrying until you get back."

"Me, too," Marta said, "but I trust Jim Cunningham's judgment." She handed Milton his backpack. "And I trust you'll use your head and not do anything foolish."

"I won't," Milton said, slipping his arms through the straps of his backpack. "Jeez! this weighs a ton. There must be enough food in here to feed an army."

"You may work up a bigger appetite than you think," Marta said. "Now, get going before Mrs. Larsen and I change our minds."

Milton and Katie walked out to their starting point at the end of the driveway. "Okay," Milton said, studying the compass, "I say our first point to navigate to is that dead pine tree at the base of the hill over there."

Katie took the compass from him. Milton had already shown Katie everything that Mr. Cunningham had taught him about using a map and compass. They had both decided they would check each other's sightings. "I agree," Katie said, handing the compass back to Milton.

They crossed the highway, headed into the forest where they immediately had a problem.

"I can't see the dead tree anymore," Katie said. "Should we keep going? I don't think we could miss it."

Milton shook his head. "We need to do everything by the book. Who knows if we'll find half a dozen dead trees once we get to the base of the hill."

They returned to their starting point and chose a closer tree to navigate toward, one that they could keep in sight as they walked. When they reached the tree, Milton again got out his compass. "Next, we head for that tree there," he said, pointing up the hill.

"Which one?" Katie said.

Milton looked up from his compass. "They all sort of look the same, don't they?" He sighed. "This is harder than it looks on paper."

"I've got an idea," Katie said. "*I'll* be the point to navigate to. I'll hike on up to those trees, and when I get there, you can tell me if I should move left or right."

"That's brilliant!"

When Katie reached the trees, Milton again sighted through his compass then waved Katie to the left. When she went too far, he waved her back right before signaling her to stop.

"Don't move," he yelled as he hiked through the woods to join her. "That's a great way to navigate through a forest as dense as this."

"Yeah, but at this rate it's gonna take us a week to get to Slick Rock."

"Not necessarily. From here, we can see most of the way to the top of the hill."

"Okay," Katie said. "This time you walk ahead while I use the compass."

Milton went as far as he could and still see Katie. He thought he was on course, but Katie had to direct him way to the left.

"I can see why a person could easily get lost without a compass," Milton said, when Katie joined him.

"I should've been guiding you as you went ahead."

"Well, I'm betting our next landmark is that large rock outcropping atop the hill."

Katie used the compass. "Close, but no cigar. It's actually that big tree to the right of it."

Milton took the compass and double checked. "I could've sworn it was going to be the outcropping. Anyway, there's nothing to block our view of it, so we can go on together."

As they climbed they couldn't hear a sound, save for the occasional snap of a twig under their boots.

"It sure is quiet," Katie said.

"Yeah, I don't think we can even hear the highway from here."

"Are you scared?"

"A little, but I'm also having fun."

"Me, too."

When they reached the tree, they found the forest beyond less dense due to a fire that had swept through years before. This allowed them to continue on together. As they became more familiar with the compass' use, they felt less anxious about getting farther and farther from the highway. Eventually, they emerged from the forest into a large meadow.

"Hey!" Milton exclaimed, "this must be Hansen's meadow. We saw it on the map." He dug his map out of his backpack and pointed to the route he had penciled in. It ran across one end of the meadow. "We're doing it, Katie! We're actually finding our way across country!"

"This meadow is so beautiful. Let's rest here a while."

They took off their backpacks and sat upon the grass.

"I've lived here my whole life and never knew this meadow existed," Katie said.

"According to the map, there's a dirt road that comes in–"

"Milton, look!"

Across the meadow, three bucks had stepped from out of the trees.

"Wow! look at the antlers on that big one," Milton exclaimed. "They're huge!"

"Not so loud. We don't want to scare them."

They sat very still and watched as the deer cautiously moved farther out into the meadow.

"Remember what I said about walking along the logging roads?" Milton said.

"About feeling like you were in a zoo?"

"Well, I don't feel that way now. I'm right here among the animals."

They drank some water and nibbled on some trail mix. As they prepared to continue on, the deer looked up, but did not run away. Leaving the meadow, they entered a forest dense with trees. Once again they were forced to go slow as one of them had to go ahead to establish a point to navigate to. Yet they were well rewarded for their diligence, for when they reached the top of another steep hill they found themselves on the edge of a wide plateau, and rising out of it the granite dome known as Slick Rock.

"Katie, we did it!"

Katie took Milton's hand and gave it a squeeze then held onto it as she and Milton admired the grandeur of the granite dome. "I guess, at this point. we could go back home."

"No way!" Milton said, and pulling Katie by the hand, began to run.

Katie laughed. "Aren't we going to take another sighting?"

"No need," Milton answered, which was true, for with the exception of a few scattered trees, the way was open before them. They ran like two young deer, bounding over rocks and downed logs, until, exhausted, they had to stop.

"Oh, my lungs!" Katie said, holding her hands over her chest.

Milton rested with hands on his knees. But that only made him dizzy, so he stood up and walked about. "I guess I should take running laps in PE more seriously."

"It's also the altitude. At lunch, let's look at the map and see how high we are."

"Do you want to eat lunch here or on top of the dome?"

"Definitely, on top."

Slick Rock was not as slick as its name implied. Neither was it too steep to walk up, and the exfoliating layers of granite created steps along with benches where they could sit and rest. As they climbed, they were able to look above the nearby ridges and off into the distance. When they reached the top, a distant range of spires lay before them with Broken Arrow being the tallest.

"Wow! what a view." Milton exclaimed. "You can see forever from up here."

"Milton, look!"

Milton looked where Katie pointed. Far off toward the southwest, a section of the highway could be seen through the trees.

"So much for getting lost," he said. He turned about. "I think Round Lake is over that ridge to the southeast." He sat down and got out his map to check. "The map shows that Round Lake is almost directly between us and Broken Arrow." He looked up and pointed. "All those jagged peaks to the left of Broken Arrow are called the Sawtooth Range."

"What's that tall peak way off to the north?" Katie said, pointing.

Milton looked at his map. "This map doesn't go that far. I see I'm going to have to get some more maps." He folded his map and exchanged it for sandwiches from his pack. "What did you bring to drink?"

"Mom packed a couple of bottles of fruit juice." She pulled the juices from her pack. "Milton, feel how tight this plastic bottle is. It feels like it's about to explode."

"It's because of the altitude. I forgot to check how high we are." He began to get the map back out of his pack.

"Do it later," Katie said. "Let's just have our lunch and enjoy the view."

Nothing could have improved upon the scenery. The writer in Milton tried to think of words to describe it. "Looking at those mountain peaks is like staring into a campfire."

"What do you mean?"

"Haven't you ever noticed how looking into a fire, or sitting by a stream, watching the water flowing by is…" He tapped his chin. "What's the word?"

"Hypnotic?"

"Exactly! I feel like someone has cast a spell over me. I want to just sit and stare forever."

Katie reached across Milton and into his pack for the map. As she studied it, Milton looked over her shoulder. "What are you looking for?"

"I just wanted to see if any of the other peaks have names. None of the peaks in the Sawtooth Range has one."

"We should name them. That tall one way at the north end of the range is now Larsen Peak."

"And the one just to the south is Mount Mickelsen. I like the sound of that. It has good alliteration."

"See that one just to the left of that gap?" Milton said.

"You mean the one that looks like a rotten tooth?"

"Right. Let's call that Mount Droshky." They both laughed.

"Can you see that peak off in the distance past Mount Droshky?" Milton said. "That has to be Mount Jeffers. The map says it's 12,412 feet high. That's almost as high as Broken Arrow."

"Maybe someday we'll climb it."

"That would be fun, though I'm not sure I'd want to if we have to use ropes and climbing gear." He told Katie about Karl Kastorsky climbing Broken Arrow.

"Rudy climbs too, you know."

"Really?"

"He doesn't talk about it much."

"That's unusual. He brags about everything."

"He's entered the science fair, you know."

"Yeah, I heard. I wonder what his project will be? The science of being a jerk?"

"Someone said it had something to do with sports."

"Why am I not surprised?"

Milton looked at Mount Jeffers. "Hey! I wonder."

"What?"

Milton got out a pencil and ruler out of his pack along with the compass.

"What are you doing?"

"Mr. Cunningham mentioned about being able to find your location using triangulation. I want to see if I can triangulate off of Mount Jeffers and Broken Arrow."

"Can I help?"

"Sure. Give me the direction toward both peaks."

Katie sighted with the compass. "Broken Arrow is fifty-six degrees east-northeast, and Mount Jeffers is…two degrees north-northeast.

"Fifty-six and two. Okay, let me see the compass." Using the compass and the directions Katie had given him, Milton plotted two courses on the map, one running from Broken Arrow and one from Mount Jeffers. Where the two lines intersected was right at Slick Rock.

"Wow!" Katie said, "that's amazing."

Milton nodded. "If you have a map and compass and can triangulate off two known points, you'll never be lost. We've got to include that in the 'science of navigation.'"

"I think we've learned a lot today."

"Yeah," Milton said, folding up the map. "And none of it was boring."

Katie tapped Milton on the leg. "I'm glad you moved to Indian Falls, Milton."

"What made you say that?"

"Well, for one, I'd never have thought of doing what we've done today."

Milton nodded. "It's been fun." He realized that, for the first time, he was really glad he had moved to Indian Falls too.

Katie began to pack away the remnants of lunch. "I suppose we should start back. Might as well not worry my mom longer than we have to."

"Should we go a different route?"

"I'd like to see Hansen's meadow again. Maybe we'll see some more deer."

Milton handed Katie the compass. "Okay, which way?"

"Well, it will be in the exact opposite direction to the way we came." She studied the compass then pointed. "It's that way."

Milton shoulder his pack. "Let's go!"

"Aren't you going to double check?"

"Nope. I think we've both mastered the use of a compass."

Chapter 17

Not wanting to explain how exactly he had let certain victory slip from his grasp, Ramblin' Red galloped out of the corral and did not stop until well away from the crowd. He dismounted outside the sheriff's office and led Cricket to the nearby horse trough. While Cricket drank, he considered what he was going to do now that Mexico was out of the picture. It was while he stood, thinking, that the lady in lavender appeared, only now attired in a plain, white dress.

"Hello, cowboy."

The last thing Ramblin' Red wanted was to have to make conversation.

But the lady continued. "I just came from watching the contest. I'm sorry you lost."

Ramblin' Red shrugged. "You know what they say, ma'am: 'You can't win 'em all.'"

The lady walked up to Cricket and began to scratch him above his nose. "You know, I've always been interested in hands, for I believe they tell a lot about a person. While everyone was watching as you raced after that steer, I was studying your hands."

Not wishing to hear another word, Ramblin' Red quickly gathered up Cricket's reins.

But the lady stayed him with a hand upon his arm. "Please, I did not mean to embarrass you, but I know you chose to lose that contest on purpose."

"And why would I do that?"

"You know very well why, and I thought it noble of you."

Ramblin' Red shook his head. "Plumb stupid, more like."

"Not to those four hungry boys." The lady released his arm but remained standing close. "I'm new to the West," she said, "and I find the people here rather…" She tapped her chin as she sought the right word.

It irritated Ramblin' Red that the lady might wish to badmouth western folk, which irritated him more, for the last thing he wanted to feel was annoyance toward this attractive woman. "I imagine folks here are the same as everywhere else."

"Oh, but they're not!" She stared down the street where music and laughter were pouring out of the saloons. "Back in New York City, where I've spent my last few years, people were always saying one thing, but doing another. But people here do what they say, and I like that. I like people who are straight forward." She turned to meet his eyes. "But you, cowboy, I think, are not so straight forward. You're a mystery, and I find that… interesting."

Ramblin' Red swallowed hard. She found him interesting, but not straight forward. Did that mean she liked him or not?

As if to assure him, the lady laid her hand upon his. At her touch, Ramblin' Red felt something he had never felt before, a simultaneous urge to run and to stay put.

The lady took her hand away. "But I talk too much, and I can see you are weary. I only wanted to learn your name so that I could stop calling you cowboy."

Ramblin' Red gave her a tired smile. "My name's Max Schaefer, though most folks call me Ramblin' Red."

"I see. Well, for the time being, I shall call you Mr. Schaefer." She stepped back. "I hope to see you again, Mr. Schaefer."

Ramblin' Red tipped his hat as she turned away. By the time he realized he had failed to ask her name in return, she was gone. He had also forgotten to return her handkerchief. From his pocket, he drew the handkerchief, which gave off the scent of lavender. He noticed the initials "LS" stitched onto one corner. He toyed with the idea of what those initials might stand for. "Lizzie Smith"? "Lizzie," to his way of thinking, did not fit with the lady's demeanor, which was... what? Serious? Refined? He shook his head. No, the lady was self-assured. It described the way she spoke her mind, the way she had held her own during the shooting contest, the way she always looked a man square in the eye, but with a special twinkle, which spoke of seeing the humor behind life's seriousness.

Perhaps the lady's name was Lavender. Ramblin' Red did not think "Lavender" any more fitting than "Lizzie,' but it would explain the lady's choice of perfume and the color of the dress she had worn earlier. Ramblin' Red liked lavender–the smell, at any rate–and should it turn out that the lady's name was Lavender, then he would come to like the name as well. He pressed the handkerchief to his nose and inhaled deeply.

It was at that moment that the sheriff chose to clear his throat.

Ramblin' Red spun about and saw Sheriff Roswell leaning against a porch post not twenty feet away. "How long you been standing there, Sheriff?"

"Oh... not long. I heard some voices and came out to investigate." The sheriff pushed away from the post. "That's when I saw you talking to our new sawbones."

Ramblin' Red shook his head. "You're mistaken, Sheriff. I was talking to a lady I'd met earlier, only being a dunderhead, I didn't get her name."

The sheriff grinned. "Her name's Laura Sutcliffe. Doctor Laura Sutcliffe, and she's our new sawbones."

Chapter 18

"If I had known how much work this was going to be," Katie said, "I would've told you to choose another subject for the science fair. Maybe something to do with sports."

Milton smiled. "I guess that comes from choosing a subject that has a few thousand years of history."

"I think I have a good idea for showing a timeline," Katie said, moving away from the large table in her family room where she and Milton had been working. She brought out a large circle, cut from piece of white poster board, and laid it on the table. "I thought in the center we could put a round map of the world drawn the way the early navigators thought it was. Then around the edges put little lines like on a compass, only instead of degrees, put the dates of significant developments in the history of navigation."

"That's brilliant!" Milton exclaimed. "Maybe if there's enough room, we could put constellations like this." Milton pulled from his backpack a planisphere, a circular map of the night sky. "The way this works is you spin the face around to reveal constellations you can see at different times of the year."

"That's cool!" Katie said. "Where'd you get it?"

"Grandma used it back when she took a course in astronomy." Milton looked at what they had collected so far. They had a sextant, a navigational tool used by sailors (lent to Katie by her uncle), the planisphere, and the compass Mr. Cunningham had given him along with several topographical maps purchased by Milton with money from his savings. "I wish we could get a real ship's chronometer," he said.

"We can fake it with a pocket watch," Katie said.

"We'll need two. One for our time here, and another showing Coordinated Universal Time."

Then there was the matter of a global positioning satellite device. "I don't know anyone who has a GPS, do you?" Milton said.

"Not to lend. They're kind of expensive."

"It'd be cool if we could get one, though. We could even do a geo-cache right there at school."

Katie shook her head. "We can't have someone wandering off with an expensive GPS unit while we're busy manning our exhibit."

"I still want to do our compass stuff, though." This was to be one of the special features of their Science of Navigation exhibit, a hands-on activity where the participant would be able to learn to use a compass to find "treasures" hidden about the multipurpose room where the science fair was to take place.

Katie's mother came into the room. "Milton, Marta is here to pick you up."

"Thanks Mrs. Larsen. I'll be right there. I just have to pack up my things."

"I'll start working on the timeline," Katie said, as she watched Milton put the things he brought into his backpack. "There's some great graphics I can get off the internet."

"And I got a book out of the school library with information about John Harrison's chronometer. I'll write up a fact sheet about how it was used to determine longitude."

"We still haven't done anything about celestial navigation."

"I know. But there's still time. We've got three more weeks."

As Milton got into the truck, Marta started the engine. "You two sure have been working hard," she said. "That's the third time you've gotten together this week."

"The science of navigation is a big topic."

"Well, I just hope you're not ignoring your other school work," Marta said, pulling out onto the highway. "I don't suppose you've had any time for your writing."

"Actually, I wrote some last night before I went to bed. Mr. Cunningham suggested I should introduce a 'love interest' into my story."

"Love interest? What do you know about a love interest?" Marta gave Milton a sharp look. "I want to hear what you wrote."

Milton got out his writing pad and read about the meeting of Ramblin' Red and Dr. Laura Sutcliffe outside the sheriff's office.

"Well, that's not so bad," Marta said, when Milton had finished. "I like the way Ramblin' Red thinks about Dr. Sutcliffe, the way he admires her assuredness without going gaga over her eyes, her lips, her slender waist, and all that lurid nonsense a boy your age shouldn't be writing about anyway. It shows that Ramblin' Red is a gentleman concerned with what's truly important in a person." Marta slowed to pull into her driveway. "Tell me, how old do you think Ramblin' Red is?"

Milton shrugged. "It's not something I've really thought about."

Marta stopped the truck near to the cabin and turned off the engine. "Well, think about it for a second."

Milton watched as a gray squirrel ran along the deck railing. "In order to get a reputation for rambling, he'd have to have been a lot of places, and that takes a lot of time, so he'd have to be pretty old. I'd say–"

Marta wagged a finger at him. "If I were you, I'd be very careful about the next words to come out of your mouth."

Milton grinned. "I mean *really* old. Thirty-five, at least, maybe even be forty, but that would make him positively *ancient*."

Marta landed a punch on his arm.

"Ow!"

She ignored his complaint. "So how old do you see Dr. Sutcliffe being?"

Milton rubbed his arm. "I've always imagined her coming west right out of medical school."

"So, she'd be all of about twenty-six or seven?"

"Maybe not even that old. I don't think it took so long to get a doctor's degree back then."

Marta sighed.

"What?"

"How come in all these stories it's always the man that's a lot older than the woman?"

"That's just the way it is."

"Well, someday I'd like to read a story where the young man falls in love with an older woman. You should write one like that. It would certainly be a lot more interesting than the young maiden falling head-over-heels for an old geezer."

"Ramblin' Red is not an old geezer."

"You know what I mean." Marta watched as Milton slid his writing pad back into his backpack. "Now that we're sort of on the subject, may I ask whether working together on your project is the only thing you are Katie are doing?"

"What do you mean?"

"I mean Katie is a lovely girl, and you're reaching that age when you might be thinking about a girlfriend."

"Jeez! Grandma, we're studying navigation not–"

"Yes, and going on outings together out in the woods. I just trust you'll always be a gentleman, and remember there'll be plenty of time for dating and such things when you're older."

"I don't believe this!" Milton exclaimed, pushing open the passenger door of the truck. "I'm going to my room and read about John Harrison." But when he got to his room, he could not stop thinking about what his grandmother had said. He realized he did have feelings for Katie that were more than just friendship. He recalled the few times he and Katie had held hands. It had made him feel special, wanted, regarded.

He shook his head. What was he thinking? He was not special. If anything, he was unexceptional. Worse, he was a runt, a squirt, no taller than boys half his age. His grandmother had it all wrong. It wasn't about his being a gentleman with Katie. It was that, being a runt, he would never get the chance.

But how great it would be to be someone tall and handsome, someone like Ramblin' Red. Thinking thus, he got out paper and pencil.

Chapter 19

Morning is one of the better times to be in the desert, standing atop a mesa, looking out over the vast empty plains where distant buttes and spires rise up like islands out of a sea. And the smell! Mornings in the desert always smell like something good is baking.

"And whole lot better than the smell of these here beans," Ramblin' Red said to no one in particular. He scraped the last of the beans out of the can then threw the can off into the bushes. The remains in his coffee pot he poured over the coals of his small campfire. The night before, he had ridden a couple of miles out of town before, feeling very tired, he stopped and spread out his bedroll not far from the road. Now as he gathered up his gear, Cricket, who had been watching, came trotting over to where his saddle rested atop a boulder.

"Morning, old fella," Ramblin' Red said, giving Cricket a pat. "I trust you slept better than I did."

Ramblin' Red flung a saddle blanket over Cricket's back, followed by the saddle. As he tightened the cinch he said, "Where shall we ramble to today?"

Cricket pricked up his ears at something over Ramblin' Red's shoulder. Ramblin' Red turned to see a fast-approaching stagecoach, backed by the rising sun.

"I'd say that driver is itching to get somewhere in a hurry, wouldn't you, Cricket?"

The driver seemed more than just 'itching.' Yet even as the stagecoach leaped and lurched over the rough road, the driver, lashing the reins over the backs of the horses, demanded more speed.

"Either he's attempting to set some kind of speed record, or he's trying to get himself killed!"

The driver was so intent upon whipping up his poor horses, he failed to notice Ramblin' Red and Cricket looking on. Yet Ramblin' Red had time to study the driver and what he saw made the hairs rise up on the back of his neck.

"That ain't no regular driver!" he declared. "That's Kid Torkasky! How on earth did he get loose?"

The curtain parted in the stagecoach door, and a face, white as a sheet, peered out.

"That's Doctor Sutcliffe!" Ramblin' Red exclaimed. "How the…" He wasted no more words, but leaped upon Cricket's back. The stagecoach had a good lead, but Cricket was fresh, while the horses pulling the stagecoach were not. Yet when the stagecoach topped a hill and started down the other side, the horses appeared to double their speed.

"Faster, Cricket!" Ramblin' Red yelled. "Faster, boy!"

A rope, the one used to secure baggage atop the stagecoach, suddenly snaked out over the back, and the stagecoach began to shed its load. A large trunk landed with a bang directly onto the road. Only a horse like Cricket, versed in the tricks of cantankerous steers, could have avoided crashing into it.

"Good boy," Ramblin' Red cried, as Cricket regained his stride. The stagecoach continued to shed more baggage. Undaunted, Cricket flew across the obstacle course of scattered clothing, dry goods and mail, which freed Ramblin' Red to concentrate upon how he was going to rescue Dr. Sutcliffe from the speeding stagecoach. As he was formulating a plan, he saw the door of the stagecoach swing open and Dr. Sutcliffe appear, poised to jump. At the speed the stage coach was traveling, jumping could only result in certain injury, perhaps death, yet she must have reasoned it better to die than remain the captive of Kid Torkasky.

Desperate to let the doctor know he was rushing to help, Ramblin' Red brought two fingers to his lips and whistled. His whistle was shrill enough to make Cricket fold back his ears, but otherwise went unheeded over the rattle and bang of the stagecoach.

Ramblin' Red jammed his boot heels into Cricket's side, and that magnificent animal responded with a burst of speed that brought Ramblin' Red close enough to the stagecoach for him to be heard when again he whistled. The look of joy upon the doctor's face upon seeing Ramblin' Red was quickly replaced by one of grim determination. She shook her head, rejecting his offer of rescue.

It took but an instant for Ramblin' Red to understand why. Laura Sutcliffe was a doctor who had chosen to dedicate her life for the good of others. She could not allow Ramblin' Red to risk injuring himself in an attempted rescue.

But just as she prepared to jump, the stagecoach bumped against a giant ponderosa tree that struck the half-open door, shattering it into fragments that rained upon Ramblin' Red. It was only through a superhuman effort that he managed to stay in the saddle. Yet he had only passed from the frying pan into the fire, for a bullet suddenly whizzed past his ear. As Ramblin' Red moved to shield himself and Cricket behind the stagecoach, Kid Torkasky fired again. Where the bullet went Ramblin' Red did not know, nor little cared, for his thoughts were upon Dr. Sutcliffe who had been knocked back inside the stagecoach.

He pushed Cricket until they were right up against the back of the stagecoach. Standing on the stirrups, he reached up, grabbed a corner of the top rail used to hold baggage atop the stagecoach then swung himself out of the saddle and onto the stagecoach's rear boot. Dangling by one hand he pulled his pistol from his holster with the other. His plan was to surprise the Kid and hopefully disarm him.

But when Ramblin' Red peered over the edge of the coach, he was shocked to see the driver's box empty. He immediately holstered his pistol, pulled himself onto the roof of the stagecoach and began to crawl forward. At that moment, the stagecoach bounded over a large rock, and suddenly Ramblin'

Red was airborne. Only a lightning grab of the top rail saved him, but left him dangling over the side of the stagecoach with nothing but air between himself and the rocky ground over which the stagecoach sped. Ramblin' Red stole a glance forward and saw the horses breaking away from the stagecoach. Somehow Kid Torkasky had managed to unhitch the horses from the stagecoach and, riding the back of one of the horses, the Kid thumbed his nose at Ramblin' Red as he and the horses disappeared over a ridge.

Ramblin' Red had no time for an angry retort, for he saw the stagecoach, without someone to guide it, was rushing headlong toward a massive rock outcropping. Hand over hand, he pulled himself along the railing until his feet were directly over the stagecoach door opposite the broken one. He swung down through the opening and landed inside. The doctor was seated on the floor, looking dazed, but otherwise uninjured. Ramblin' Red swept her up and prepared to jump through the opening left by the absent door. He figured if he were to land upon his back, he would bear the brunt of the impact and perhaps save the doctor from major injury.

But just as he was about to sacrifice himself, Cricket appeared alongside the stagecoach. Without hesitation, Ramblin' Red, with Dr. Sutcliffe in his arms, leaped from the stagecoach and onto Cricket's back. It was not a moment too soon, for as Cricket veered away, the stagecoach slammed into the rocks and was smashed to smithereens.

Cricket slowed to a walk then stopped. Ramblin' Red eased the doctor down to the ground where she lay as one dead. Ramblin' Red himself was so exhausted he could barely manage to stay in the saddle. He slipped to the ground and sat with his head between his legs while the world seemed to revolve around him. Eventually he managed to crawl over to Dr. Sutcliffe who still lay unmoving.

"Dr. Sutcliffe," he said in a hoarse voice. He gently shook her by the arm.

She moaned, turned over and looked up Then her eyes lit up in recognition of her savior, and she flung her arms around Ramblin' Red and cried upon his chest. Bits of phrases poured forth. "…thought I was going to die… he was handcuffed to the hospital bed… must have got loose… scalpel to my throat… me hostage… the guard's gun… stole the stagecoach… said he'd shoot me if…."

"There, there," Ramblin' Red said, running his fingers through her hair. "It's over now. You're safe."

When the doctor had cried herself out, Ramblin' Red offered her a handkerchief. She dried her eyes then offered the handkerchief back.

"It actually belongs to you," Ramblin' Red said.

Dr. Sutcliffe noticed the initials. "Oh!" she said, with a little laugh. "So it does." She tucked the handkerchief under the sleeve of her dress. "Would you help me up, please, Mr. Schaefer? I'm still a little shaky."

Ramblin' Red stood up on wobbly legs. It seemed to take all his strength to help the doctor stand. They stood, gazing into each other's eyes until the doctor reached up and pulled Ramblin' Red's face toward hers, and he felt his mouth close upon her dry, chapped and wrinkled old lips.

"Jesus!" Ramblin' Red exclaimed, jumping back.

"You will not use profanity in this story!" Milton's grandmother declared. "You will limit your exclamations to 'gosh!' 'darn!' and 'golly!'"

Ramblin' Red blinked several times, but nothing changed. "Who are you, and what's become of Doctor Sutcliffe?"

"Forget the doctor! I'm your new love interest now. My grandson wrote me in."

"Who's your grandson?"

"He's the one writing this story."

"Is he, now?" Ramblin' Red squared his shoulders. "Well, I'd like to have a few words with him."

"Oh, hush!" Marta said, reaching up and placing her hand upon Ramblin' Red's rough cheek. "Now, where were we… oh, yes, the handsome young cowboy was kissing his new love, the older, but still quite attractive, Marta

Mickelsen."

Ramblin' Red gently pulled Marta's hand away. "I don't mean no disrespect, ma'am—I mean, for an older woman you're—"

Marta wagged a finger. "If I were you, I'd be very careful about the next words to come out of your mouth."

Ramblin' Red swallowed hard. "As I was saying, I mean no offense, ma'am, but I don't think your grandson has written this part right."

"Oh, phooey!" Marta said, stepping back. "Have it your own way. Besides, this is no time for romance." She pointed to his blood-soaked shirt. "Its seems you've been shot."

Ramblin' Red looked down at his shirt. "I have?"

"Afraid so."

"Well, gosh, darn, and golly!"

Chapter 20

Milton leaned on the bar that separated him from the driver's seat of the bus. "You're coming to the science fair tonight, aren't you, Mr. Cunningham?"

"I wouldn't miss it for the world, Milton. Tell me again what time it starts."

"It starts at seven, but Katie and I are going to get there at five. It's going to take some time getting everything set up. Thanks again for letting us use your other compass."

"Sure," Mr. Cunningham said, "though I still don't know why you need more than one."

Milton had not told Mr. Cunningham about the "hands-on" feature of their exhibit. "You'll see."

Marta had a snack waiting when Milton got to the cabin. "I'm too excited to eat," he said.

"Well, eat anyway. You'll need something in you to get through the evening."

Milton quickly ate the sandwich Marta had prepared then carried to the truck the exhibit materials he had carefully packed up the night before.

"I trust you're being careful with the things lent you," Marta said, as Milton came back into the cabin.

"Katie's bringing the sextant," Milton answered, "and I carefully wrapped Mr. Cunningham's compass." He looked at the clock on the fireplace mantle. "Can we go early?"

"What's the matter? You got ants in your pants?"

"There's just a lot of stuff we've got to do before the fair starts."

"All right, fetch my coat from the closet. I'll bet you won't find Katie being so antsy."

But Katie was already at the school when they arrived. She helped Milton carry his boxes into the multipurpose room where her materials were already on the table they had been assigned.

"If it's all right," Marta said, "I'll leave you kids to do what you have to do while I go to the market."

With Marta gone, they had the multipurpose room to themselves.

"Quick!" Milton said. "Let's hide the candy."

"There's not a lot of places to hide things in here," Katie responded.

Still, they were able to hide about thirty pieces of candy before the other contestants began to arrive. While their peers were setting up their exhibits, Milton and Katie wrote on slips of paper the location, in degrees on the compass, of each piece of candy they had hidden. This took longer than they planned. They barely got their exhibit set up in time for the science fair to begin. Milton and Katie stood beneath a banner Katie had made: *The Treasure Hunt Starts Here!*

An eighth-grader Milton only knew by sight was the first visitor to their exhibit. "What do you mean, 'Treasure Hunt'?"

"One of the most common ways of navigating is by using a compass," Milton said, picking up one of the compasses.

Katie handed the eighth-grader one of the slips of paper with coordinates written on it. "If you follow these coordinates, you'll find a treasure somewhere in this room."

"Cool!" the eighth-grader said. "So, how do I use a compass?"

Katie and Milton showed him. "Your treasure is located somewhere in line with the direction of your coordinates," Milton said.

The eighth-grader sighted through the compass. "I bet the treasure's up there on the stage," he said, and went off to find it.

"Can I try?" Brenda Miller said. She had been listening while Katie and

Milton had been instructing the eighth-grader on the compass' use.

"Me, too!" said Kate, Brenda's younger sister.

Katie looked at Milton. "I guess that's why we needed two compasses."

Soon other students were lining up to become treasure seekers. "At this rate, all the treasures will be found before the science fair is even half over," Milton said.

"Maybe that's just as well," Katie said, handing another participant a slip of paper. "Nobody's looking at the rest of our exhibit."

"I bet that lady will," Milton said, pointing to a woman who was studying a nearby exhibit and making notes on a clipboard. "She must be one of the judges."

"I know her," Katie said. "She works for the forestry with my dad. I think she's a wildlife biologist."

When the judge came to their exhibit, she spent a long time reading all the information that Milton and Katie had compiled.

"This is very impressive," she said. "I particularly like the way you've presented your timeline, and the way you've explained how the navigational tools work. But can you do more than just explain them? Can you actually use the navigational tools yourself?"

Katie picked up the sextant and demonstrated its use. "By taking a noontime sighting of the sun and calculating its angle…" she pointed to an illustration she had made for the exhibit, "a sailor could determine his latitude."

"And once Harrison developed an accurate chronometer," Milton added, "a navigator could determine longitude by comparing his time at noon with that of his chronometer set at Coordinated Universal Time."

The judge nodded. "And I see you're doing something with compasses."

Milton pointed to the people waiting to go treasure hunting. "We've hidden small treasures about the room and are showing people how to use a compass to find them. It's pretty basic navigation, not like when we're actually out in the field."

The judge smiled. "And have you actually been in the field?"

Katie and Milton explained how they used point-to-point navigation to go from Milton's cabin to Slick Rock.

"I see," the judge said. "So you must have passed through a meadow on your way."

"Hansen's!" Milton and Katie answered in unison.

"It's beautiful!" Katie said.

"We saw several bucks," Milton added. "One with a huge rack."

"I think I know the buck you're talking about," the judge said. "I'm doing a deer population study in that area."

"Hey!" Juan Ortiz interrupted. "Are we going to hunt for treasure or what?"

"I'll let you get back to what you were doing," the judge said. She made some notes on her clipboard before moving along to the next exhibit.

By six-thirty, most of the pieces of candy had been found.

"Let's make this the last treasure seeker," Milton said, handing a slip of paper to yet another participant. "Almost all the pieces have been found except the one we're saving for Mr. Cunningham."

Miss Droshky stopped to look at their exhibit. She read through the information without comment.

"Care to go on a treasure Hunt, Miss Droshky?" Katie said.

Miss Droshky shook her head and moved along to the next exhibit.

"What's with her?" Milton said "She didn't say a word!"

"And this whole science fair was her idea. You'd think she'd show a little enthusiasm for it."

Next to come by was Mrs. Reese, the principal. "I hear you've been sending people off to hunt for treasure. Only you two and one other contestant have been offering a hands-on experience."

"Who's that?" Katie said.

"Rudy Kastorsky. He has an excellent exhibit on the science of wilderness survival."

Milton and Katie looked over to where Rudy was wrapping someone's arm with a t-shirt.

"What's he doing?" Milton said.

"It looks like he's showing how to put a person's arm in a sling," Katie answered.

"That's science?" Milton said.

"Medicine is certainly science," Mrs. Reese said, "and there's much more to his exhibit than just his hands-on activities. You'll both have to go and see what the other contestants have done. All in all, I'd say that this science fair has been a resounding success."

"You want to go look around?" Milton said to Katie, once Mrs. Reese had moved on.

"We could both go. Now that we're not doing any more treasure hunting there's really no need for us to stay here."

"I think one of us should stay here and guard against someone stealing something," Milton said.

"That's the city boy talking. No one here is going to steal anything."

"Yeah, well, I still want to be here when Mr. Cunningham comes."

As if on cue, Mr. Cunningham arrived. "So how's it going, you two?" he said.

"Great!" Milton answered.

They waited while Mr. Cunningham looked over their exhibit. "You two have really outdone yourself," he said. "This is very informative. And the graphics on your presentation are excellent."

"That's Katie's work," Milton said. "She's the one that's the artist."

"You should hang on to your work, Katie," Mr. Cunningham said, "especially that timeline. If it were me, I'd have it framed. Now, what's all this I've heard about a treasure hunt."

"That's why we had to have the other compass," Milton said.

"We thought the treasure hunting would be a popular feature," Katie said.

"At one point we had a long line of people waiting," Milton said. "We could have used a dozen compasses."

"But there was only the two of us to show how they worked," Katie added.

"Is it too late for me to try my luck?" Mr. Cunningham said.

"We've saved one just for you," Milton said, handing Mr. Cunningham a slip of paper with coordinates on it.

Mr. Cunningham took the paper then picked up a compass and began to put it to use. "Ah! I see you're going to make me go outside the multipurpose room. Do I have to hike to Timbuktu, or might my treasure be in the planter just outside the door?"

Both Milton and Katie laughed.

"I'll take your laughter to mean it's in the planter. We'll then, I guess I better go find it. By the way, you should go look at Rudy Kastorsky's exhibit. He's really done a good job."

"That's what we've heard," Katie said.

"I can't believe a jerk like Rudy could do a good job!" Milton muttered, once Mr. Cunningham had left.

"Well, let's go find out," Katie said.

Chapter 21

Milton and Katie found Rudy lecturing to a small group of onlookers. "Hypothermia can be a killer, especially if you're unprepared for the cold." He pointed to one of his displays. "This shows the stages of hypothermia starting with uncontrollable shivering all the way to loss of consciousness and cardiac arrhythmias." He picked up a sweater off his table. "One of the best ways to keep warm is to wear wool. It has natural oils, which help to shed water and provide warmth even when wet.

"Another killer is an untreated injury, like a broken bone." He picked up two long pieces of tree bark. "Even out in the middle of the wilderness, you can find something to use to make a simple splint. Now, can I have a volunteer?"

While Rudy demonstrated on a little boy how to stabilize a broken bone using bark and strips of cloth torn from a T-shirt, Milton looked over the rest of Rudy's exhibit. Not only was there the information about hypothermia, there was another display depicting types of common wilderness injuries, illustrated with photos and with a clear scientific explanation as to why these can be life threatening. He even had some rescue equipment borrowed from the local search and rescue organization.

Though Milton hated to admit it, Rudy had really done an excellent job, and he worried that the judges might find Rudy's exhibit better than Katie and his.

But to Milton's way of thinking, the best science fair exhibit was on the subject of transportation done by an eighth-grader named Lionel Holloway. Lionel had dozens of working models of different modes of transportation; everything from dog sleds to stagecoaches to automobiles to the Space Shuttle

Discovery. Not only that, he had models with cutaway views showing the inner workings of many types of engines, from steam engines to ones run on nuclear power. He even had an actual car engine that had been cut in half to reveal its inner parts, all carefully labeled.

"This is incredible," Milton said.

"Thanks," Lionel said, "I've been working on this stuff for years."

"And you made all these models?"

Smiling, Lionel nodded.

"You must have started like when you were five years old."

Lionel pointed to a model of a Native American riding a horse pulling a travois. "I actually made this one when I was only four."

"Well, this is definitely the best exhibit in the fair."

"Thanks. It's given me the chance to share my passion. Someday I'm going to be a mechanical engineer."

Milton stared down the three tables required to display Lionel's exhibit. "But how are you going to get all this stuff in the van when you go to the Exploratorium?"

Lionel laughed. "There's no way all this will fit in a van. We've got a trailer that my dad's going to drive."

They were interrupted by an announcement over the PA system. "If I could have your attention, please," said the voice of Mrs. Reese. "As you can see by the clock, it's getting time to bring our evening's activity to a close. I'm sure I speak for all when I say that our students have done a wonderful job, educating us about science. Let's give them a big hand!"

During the applause, Milton and Katie returned to their exhibit.

"I'd like to thank our panel of judges who have so graciously given of their time tonight and to ask one of our judges, Sue Cuomo, to come and announce the winners of tonight's competition."

Sue Cuomo, the judge who had talked earlier to Milton and Katie, came to the microphone. "I know I speak for all of the judges when I say how difficult it was to decide upon the winners. You all did incredible jobs, and deserve another round of applause." As the audience again applauded, Sue unfolded a piece of paper. "Here are the finalists who will represent McKinley Middle School at the Exploratorium. The winners in the eighth-grade division are Lionel Holloway and Rebecca Berkowitz."

"Are you nervous?" Milton said to Katie, as the audience applauded the winners.

"A little. How about you?"

Milton held up a shaking hand, and Katie laughed.

"In the seventh grade, the winners are Anna Pease and Elizabeth Walters."

As the audience again applauded, Katie took Milton's hand. "Here goes," she said.

"Before I announce our last two winners let me say that there were two presentations among the sixth-graders that we thought particularly outstanding, which made it very difficult to decide who should win." She looked down at her paper. "That said, the winners in the sixth grade are Katie Larsen and Milton Mickelsen."

Katie squealed in delight as Milton jumped up and down.

"Let me just say…" Sue Cuomo waited for the applause to die. "… let me just say how impressed we were by Rudy Kastorsky's presentation on the science of wilderness survival. I think Rudy deserves his own round of applause."

Though Rudy held up his hand in acknowledgement, he did not look very happy.

"Before we close this evening, let me thank all the teachers, especially our science teacher Miss Droshky. Let's make this an annual event! Now, before any of the contestants leave tonight, be sure to see Mrs. Reese. She has a gift certificate from Chubby's Drive-in for you."

Milton and Katie pulled the boxes from under their table and began to pack things away. "We did it, Katie. All our hard work paid off."

Katie nodded.

"You don't look too happy."

"I can't help feeling sorry for Rudy. He did a really good job."

Milton shrugged. "Excuse me if I don't join you in your commiseration."

"You shouldn't be so unfeeling."

"The guy's a jerk!"

Katie turned her back on Milton as she continued packing things away.

Milton realized he had once again angered Katie. Still he could not help feeling glad Rudy was not going to the Exploratorium with them. Likely he would have spent the three-hour ride slapping Milton in the back of the head and calling him buttock. That said…

"Oh, brother!" Milton exclaimed, rubbing his forehead.

Katie turned about. "What is it?"

"I just had this really terrible idea. You know Lionel's not going in the van with us? He's got too much stuff to fit in it."

Katie smiled. "Which means there's actually room for one more." Katie looked around. "We should tell this to Miss Droshky."

"I think I'd rather tell Mrs. Reese."

"Tell me what?" Mrs. Reese said, placing two gift certificates on their table.

"Milton was saying how Lionel won't be going to the Exploratorium in the van because he's got too much stuff."

"His dad's going to take him," Milton said. "They've got a trailer."

"That means there'll be room for one more person in the van," Katie said.

Miss Droshky appeared and listened in on the conversation.

"And since Rudy did such a good job…" Milton said.

"And since the judge said they could hardly decide between him and us…" Katie added.

Miss Droshky, who saw where this was leading, shook her head. But Mrs. Reese looked pleased. "You think Rudy should go to the Exploratorium with you?" she said.

Both Milton and Katie nodded.

"I think that's a splendid idea!" Mrs. Reese said. She laid a hand upon Milton's shoulder. "And I appoint you to give Rudy the good news."

"Why me?"

"It was your idea, wasn't it?"

Milton shook his head. "How do I get myself into these things?"

"Come on," Katie said, taking Milton by the arm, "I'll go along for moral support."

They found Rudy taking down his exhibit with his dad's help. Rudy roughly tossed the two pieces of bark into a box.

"Careful, son," Karl Kastorsky said.

"Why? What does it matter? I won't be using this stuff anymore." He turned around to see Milton and Katie. "What? You come to gloat?"

"No," Katie said. "Milton has something to tell you."

Milton swallowed hard. "We thought you did a really great job, Rudy."

"Well, who asked you, anyway?"

"Rudy, mind your manners!" his father said.

But Rudy was not listening. He towered over Milton. "I don't care what you or anybody else thinks. Besides, these contests are a joke. The stupid judges are just like the stupid teachers in this stupid school. They think only certain people have any brains." Rudy poked Milton in the chest. "Like Katie-Matey and her little friend here."

Milton rubbed his chest where Rudy had poked him. "I didn't come here to…" Too angry to say more, he turned and walked away.

Katie stepped forward. "You know, Rudy, you really are a jerk! I don't know why I even bother to defend you. Milton didn't come over here to gloat. He came to tell you that you've been chosen to go to the Exploratorium with us."

"Yeah, right!" He turned away and shoved the wool sweater into a box.

"It's true!"

Rudy turned back. "And when was this decided?"

"Just now, by Mrs. Reese."

The anger disappeared from Rudy's face. "Really? No kidding?"

"No kidding."

"Well, gee, I…" Rudy looked up at his dad who now stood beside him. "Did you hear what Katie said?"

Karl Kastorsky nodded.

Rudy looked back at Katie and grinned. "Cool!"

Chapter 22

Milton felt rather blue following the science fair. His grandmother explained that this was only natural. "When you put so much effort into something, you're bound to feel a little letdown once it's over. But remember, you still have the Exploratorium to look forward to."

The idea of competing at the Exploratorium did not seem so fun now that Rudy was going along. Milton was still angry at Rudy, even though lately Rudy had not gone out of his way to torment Milton. That still did not make Milton like Rudy any more. About the only thing he found in Rudy's favor was his choice of fiction. Since being introduced to science fiction, Milton had become addicted, which made him feel guilty about abandoning westerns. He discussed this with Mr. Cunningham.

"Do you ever read anything other than westerns?" he said.

"Of course."

"Like what?"

"Well, like history."

"History about the West?"

"About all sorts of things. I also like mysteries."

"Ever read much science fiction?"

Mr. Cunningham shook his head. "Not since I was about your age."

Milton sighed.

"What's troubling you, partner?"

"Well, for one, I've not been writing much lately."

"What's the matter, writer's block?"

"No, it just seems my story has somehow gotten away from me. I'm feeling scattered and unable to focus."

"Maybe you're being too hard on yourself. We all have our little ups and downs. I'm sure you'll get back into writing soon. After all, what would the world be without Ramblin' Red?"

But in the days that followed, Milton couldn't seem to get into anything, though, for some reason, he kept thinking about the topic of the writing contest. When he was supposed to be taking notes in Miss Droshky's science class, he tried again to write an essay.

Why I Write

Milton tapped his pencil on his teeth. No great thoughts came to mind, so he decided to make a list of all the reasons he might wish to write, even if none of them were true.

1. I write because I have nothing else to do.
2. I write because it's fun.
3. I write because short people can't do anything else.
4. I write because I'm no good at sports.
5. I write because writers make big bucks, and I'm going to be rich.
6. I write because someday when I'm a published author, people will be impressed.
7. I write because I've run out of things to read.
8. I write because I have an obsessive-compulsive disorder and I can't stop putting words on paper.
9. I write because there's this little man in my head that makes me.
10. I write to make some sense of my life.

Of the ten reasons, only the last one seem to speak to him. But was it true? Did he write to make sense of his life? He liked Ramblin' Red, but there seemed little about Ramblin' Red's life that mirrored his own. Perhaps his writing was just an exercise in wishful thinking; writing about the adventures of Ramblin' Red made up for the lack of excitement in his own life. What I'd give to have my own adventure, he thought.

Katie kicked Milton's chair.

"What!" Milton shouted.

His classmates turned to stare at him.

"Here!" Milton said, holding up his notebook toward Miss Droshky. "Take it! I'll serve detention too."

Miss Droshky peered at Milton over the top of the reading glasses she wore when consulting her notes. "I don't know what you're going on about, Milton, but I'll thank not to interrupt our class. Now, getting back to the subject of anatomy…"

Katie leaned forward and whispered. "Sorry. I didn't mean to kick your chair."

Milton was in a foul mood when he got home. He slammed the door then thunked down his backpack upon the dining table.

Marta stuck her head out of the kitchen doorway. "I'll thank you not to hurt my table!" she scolded.

Milton threw himself into a living room chair and sat with arms crossed over his chest. Marta came into the living room, drying her hands on a towel. "I take it things didn't go well at school today."

Milton sat in silence.

"Well, I'll leave you to work it out by yourself," Marta said.

"Things went okay," Milton said.

Marta sat down in another chair. "So what's troubling you?"

"I don't know. Everything's just…" Milton tried to think of an appropriate metaphor. "I feel like I'm a leaf being blown around by the wind. I'm restless. I can't seem to get into anything. Sometimes I feel like I'm about to jump out of my skin. And to make matters worse, I can't seem to write. I don't know if

I even *want* to write anymore. I mean, today I made a list of all the reasons why I write, and there only one reason that was any good."

"And what one was that?"

" 'I write to make sense of my life.' "

"I believe a lot of writers write for just that reason."

"Yeah, but I always wrote because it was fun, because I like stories with a lot of action in them, because I like it when the good guy comes out on top. Writing to make sense of my life? Where's the story in that? Where's the fun?"

Marta leaned back in her chair. "I like what I'm hearing. This is good."

"I'm glad you're amused."

"No, I mean it. I think you're growing up."

"I'm not growing up, I'm growing crazy."

"No, the frustration you're feeling represents a maturity in your thinking. Remember when I said that a great writer not only writes well, but writes about something worth writing?"

Milton nodded.

"Well, I sense the frustration you're feeling is because you're no longer satisfied with what you've been writing. Stories with lots of action and good guys coming out on top are okay, but you must know by now that life is not usually like that. And if you're truly wanting to make a career in writing, you're going to have to find something to write about that will keep you and your readers interested over the long haul."

"Like what?"

"Like writing about things that are real. Things that shape your life. Things that make you who you are. That's what will appeal to your readers because, whether we realize it or not, we're all trying to make sense of our lives."

"I've been reading a lot of science fiction lately."

"Science fiction can be a lot like westerns, a lot of action and a lot of good guys always coming out on top."

"But why can't I be a writer like Harry Harrison? He made a whole career on action adventures."

"You can, if that's where your talents lie. But you must first find your own voice. Some people say that each of us is put on this earth for a purpose. I'm not really sure that's true. But there is one thing I *am* sure of, and that is there is only one Milton Mickelsen, one person with his special gifts, and it would be a shame if the world were to miss out on those gifts just because he chose to ignore them and write like someone else."

Milton did not reply, but sat thinking.

Marta stood up. "Well, I should get back to making dinner."

"But even if I do work on finding my own voice," Milton said, "I can't just desert Ramblin' Red. I mean, he's just been shot, and if I don't help him out, he's going to bleed to death."

"No, you surely mustn't let that happen."

Milton stood up. "So, maybe I'll do a little writing before dinner."

"Good! And I'll–" Marta took a sudden step back and looked Milton over. "Oh, my goodness."

"What?" Milton said.

"Tell me, how tall were you last time we measured?" she said.

"Four-eleven. Why?"

"Go stand over by the door. I want to measure you again."

While Milton went to the door, Marta got a tape measure. "Stand up straight, no slouching."

Milton pushed his back hard against the door.

"Well, now I know what part of your problem is," she said, studying the tape. "You've got growing pains."

"What do you mean?"

She held the tape so Milton could see it. "According to this, you're now five foot, two inches."

Chapter 23

Having veered away from the runaway stagecoach, Cricket slowed to a walk then stopped. Ramblin' Red eased the doctor down to the ground where she lay as one dead. Ramblin' Red himself was so exhausted he could barely manage to stay in the saddle. He slipped to the ground and sat with his head between his legs while the world seemed to revolve around him. He chastised himself for sitting there when the doctor needed his help. Yet try as he might, he could not move. He rubbed a soreness in his shoulder and brought his hand away, dripping in blood.

"Stay still!" ordered Dr. Sutcliffe, suddenly by his side.

Ramblin' Red smiled. "Why, Doctor, you're not hurt!"

"Thanks to you, I'm not. And thanks to me, you are." She fumbled with the buttons of his shirt. "Damn! I can't stop my fingers from shaking."

"You shouldn't cuss."

"Says who?"

"I dunno. I think it was some lady in a dream or something. Besides, you shouldn't fuss over a little blood. Kid Torkasky's not much of a shot. I'm sure he just nicked me."

The doctor finally managed to get Ramblin' Red's shirt open. "I'm afraid he did more than nick you." She reached down and tore off a section of her petticoat, which she used to stem the bleeding. It did little to stop the flow of blood.

Ramblin' Red closed his eyes. "I'm feeling a mite sleepy. If you don't mind, I think I might just take a little siesta."

"No! You must not go to sleep!" When Ramblin' Red did not respond, she shook his arm. "Mr. Schaefer, do you understand what I'm saying? You must not sleep!"

Ramblin' Red opened one eye. "Did you just call me 'Mr. Schaefer'? He chuckled. "I can't remember the last time someone called me Mr. Schaefer."

"You forget. I called you that last night."

"Was it just last night? Seems like ages ago." He closed his eyes once more. "You sure I can't sleep a spell?"

"Mr. Schaefer!" she shouted. "Look at me!"

Ramblin' Red's response was to drop his chin upon his chest.

"Max!" she shouted. She slapped him hard on the face. "Open your eyes and look at me!"

Slowly, Ramblin' Red raised his head and opened his eyes. "I see you, Doctor. No need to get all riled up." He smiled. "My, you're prettier than a sunlit valley."

"Oh, God, he's delirious!" She tore off another section of her petticoat and wrapped it around the blood-soaked cloth. "I need my black bag! I need proper bandages!" A sob tore from her throat. "Oh, what am I to do?"

It was just then that Nero Marceau came racing up. He was out of his saddle even before Jupiter came to a halt. "Dr. Sutcliffe! Are you all right?"

"Yes, thanks to this man. But…"

Nero stared down at the hunched over figure of Ramblin' Red and saw blood everywhere. "What do you need me to do?"

"I need–"

She was interrupted by the arrival of Sheriff Roswell. "You all right, ma'am?"

"No time for that," Dr. Sutcliffe said, taking charge. "Nero, you've got the fastest horse. I want you to race to town and get my black bag and lots of bandages. The bandages are in the cupboard above the sink."

Nero leaped into the saddle.

"No, wait!" She turned to address the sheriff. "Is there someplace nearby we can take Mr. Schaefer?"

"There's Randy Stark's place," he said. "It's just a little way up the road."

"Right!" Nero said. "I'll get what you need and meet you there."

"And you." Dr. Sutcliffe said, pointing to the sheriff. "I want you to ride as fast as you can to Stark's place and bring back a buckboard to transport Mr. Schaefer in."

The sheriff jammed his heel into the side of his horse and raced off.

"And all the blankets you can find!" Dr. Sutcliffe shouted after him.

"I'll do my best," the sheriff shouted back.

Dr. Sutcliffe turned to her patient. "How are you doing, Mr. Schaefer?"

"All right, I guess. Toes are a mite tingly." He held up a bloody hand. "Fingers, too."

"I'm afraid you've lost some blood, but don't worry, Nero and the sheriff have gone for help. All you have to do is hold on a little longer, and everything will be just fine."

Ramblin' Red nodded.

"So while we're waiting," the doctor said, "tell me a little about yourself."

"There's not much to tell, I'm afraid."

"But surely a man like you must have lived a very interesting life. Start by telling me why they call you 'Ramblin' Red'?"

He smiled. "I guess that's because I tend to wander around a bit. I can't seem to stick at one thing for long. I take a job just long enough to make a little money so I can go rambling again."

"I imagine you've seen many pretty places in your rambling."

"That I have. I've seen sunrises that color the desert like a bouquet of roses. I've seen mountains so high I got a neck ache just looking up at them. I've been down canyons so deep and mysterious they just seem like to swallow a man up. I've…" Ramblin' Red went silent.

"Tell me more," Dr. Sutcliffe said, trying to keep the worry out of her voice. "Tell me more about places you've been."

He shook his head. "I'm afraid I can't. I reckon I got no choice but to sleep awhile."

"No!" She pulled him toward her and cradled him in her arms. "Tell me about your horse. Why is he called 'Cricket'?"

"No, I got to tell you something else. Like I said, I've done a lot of rambling in my time."

"Yes, I know," she said, resting her head against his. "I want to hear more about your travels."

With a great effort, Ramblin' Red pulled away and sat up, looking into Dr. Sutcliffe's eyes. "This is important, and I got to say it while I can." He found one of her hands and took it in his. "The first time I saw you, I realized…" His eyes went glassy and he began to pitch forward.

Dr. Sutcliffe grabbed him to keep him from falling. "What, Max? What did you realize?"

Ramblin' Red raised his head and smiled. "I realized right then that I didn't want to ramble no more." Then his body went slack as he lost consciousness.

Chapter 24

The morning of the Exploratorium's science fair was so cold, Milton's breath froze on the glass as he stood looking out of his bedroom window.

"I'm afraid for you to go today," Marta said when he came down for breakfast. "It looks like a big storm is moving in."

Milton sat down at the kitchen counter. "Mr. Cunningham said that this is the latest in the year it's been without getting any snow."

Marta filled Milton's glass with orange juice. "In my experience, the longer old man winter holds back, the worse it is when he lets go. I just hope the storm holds off until you get home. I worry about Miss Droshky driving you kids in the snow."

Yet by the time Marta drove Milton to school, most of the clouds had disappeared.

"Hurry and load your stuff," Miss Droshky said, scowling at the six students who were going to the Exploratorium. "We've a long way to go."

"I see Miss Droshky is her usual cheerful self," Katie whispered to Milton, as they loaded their boxes into the rear of the van.

"That doesn't surprise me," Milton replied. What did surprise him was that Rudy actually mumbled a "good morning" to him as they were loading. Milton had been too stunned to reply.

Had Miss Droshky's driving habits been anything like her personality, they would have been in trouble. But she was a very conscientious driver, and Milton was able to relax and enjoy the scenery as they drove down the highway that bordered the canyon through which flowed Indian Creek. He wondered whether he was going to see any of the students from his old school at the science fair.

But the chances of meeting a former acquaintance seemed slim once they arrived at the Exploratorium and entered the cavernous hall in which the science fair was taking place.

"This place is gigantic!" Katie exclaimed.

"There must be a thousand kids here, at least," Milton said.

They found their assigned table and began to unpack their boxes. "We'll have to hurry," Katie said. "Most everyone else is set up already."

Since they knew they were going to be pushed for time, Milton and Katie had opted not to hide any treasures. Instead for the "hands-on" feature of their exhibit they would offer the observer the opportunity to learn how to plot a route on a map using a compass.

"This is exciting!" Katie said, once they had everything set up.

Milton looked around the hall where every inch was filled with science fair exhibits. "I don't know how they're going to be able to judge them all."

A loud voice came over the PA system. "May I have your attention, please!" The speaker, who stood on a raised platform at the far end of the hall, waited for the room to quiet. "Thank you. I am Dr. Maria Cisneros, and I am the director of the Bayside Exploratorium. On behalf of myself and the staff, we'd like to welcome you all to the Exploratorium's first-time ever, student science fair!"

The director waited for the cheering to subside. "In just a few moments, we're going to open the doors to the general public, but first I want to let you know that throughout the morning the judges will be circulating throughout the hall. Each judge will likely ask you questions about your project, so it is imperative that each station be manned at all times. If for any reason you have to leave your station—by the way, the restrooms are next to the door to my right—then raise your hand and a volunteer will come stand beside your exhibit until you return. Don't take too long! Once the judges are done, we'll let you know, and at that time you'll be free to go about and enjoy looking at the other exhibits.

"So, now if we're ready, let's open the doors and let the science fair begin!"

As the main doors were opened, a stream of people began to pour in, mostly younger students who had been bussed in for this event. Some of the little kids began to run down the rows.

"No running!" shouted a woman who looked to be their teacher.

The children slowed to a walk, but not before one of them bumped a table not far from Milton and Katie, and water spilled from one of the exhibit's jars containing oxygen-producing algae.

"Oh, great!" the exhibitor shouted.

An official, in dress and high-heels came clattering down the row to see what the trouble was. Unfortunately, she did not see the spilled water. She slipped and fell hard. She did not say anything, but it was obvious that she was hurt.

A man with a badge identifying him as a judge soon reached her. "Alice, are you all right?"

"I turned my ankle. Serves me right for wearing these stupid shoes."

Rudy appeared, clutching a roll of elastic bandages. "I'm here to help." He spoke with such authority, no one challenged him. He found a chair and helped the woman up into it. Then kneeling before her, he took the woman's ankle in his hands.

"Ouch!" she exclaimed as Rudy gently probed.

"It's not broken," Rudy said, "but we'll need some ice." He turned to the judge. "Go get some!"

"But… but…" the judge stammered.

"Now!" Rudy barked.

The judge shrugged his shoulders and turned to do as directed.

"Boy, Rudy sure knows how to take command," Katie said to Milton.

Milton nodded, amazed to see how the other adults who had arrived upon the scene had bowed to Rudy's authority.

Rudy found another chair and placed the woman's leg atop it, resting the leg on a towel that he taken from a nearby exhibitor who had used it as packing material. "R-I-C-E," Rudy said in a loud voice. "Rest, ice, compression, and elevation. Those are the treatments for a sprain."

The judge returned with a cup of ice and handed it to Rudy. Rudy looked around and not seeing what he wanted, he took off his shoe and removed his sock. "I put this on clean this morning, by the way," he said holding up the sock. He began to fill it with ice. "Ice helps reduce a swelling, but you never want to put it on the skin directly." He placed the sock over the woman's ankle.

"Clever to use your sock that way," the injured woman said.

Rudy, putting his shoe back on, addressed those around him. "You've got to know how to improvise if you're going to be out in the wilderness." He pointed toward his exhibit. "You'll find in my exhibit on wilderness medicine all sorts of common items that can be used in an emergency." He turned back to address the woman with the sprained ankle. "After the ice has been on your ankle for a while, I'll use this elastic bandage to wrap it."

"Thank you," she said, "but I can't just stay sitting here; I'm blocking the aisle."

Rudy nodded. "If we were in the wilderness, and you needed to get around, you could devise a crutch using a dead branch. Or if there were others with you, they could use a two-man carry to move you." Rudy carefully lifted the woman's leg down off the chair. "But in this case, we can simply transport you using your chair." He motioned to the judge who had brought the ice to help him. "Keep your back straight," he cautioned, as they prepared to lift the woman.

"Oh!" the woman exclaimed, as she suddenly rose into the air.

"Bring that other chair and towel, and follow us," Rudy ordered a bystander.

The bystander picked up the chair and towel and began to follow. "That kid sure knows his stuff!" he said.

"Well," Katie said, once the excitement had passed, "if that doesn't earn Rudy a prize, I don't know what will."

Milton nodded. Much as he hated to admit it, Rudy was a natural-born leader. Seeing Katie's look of admiration gave him a lump in his stomach. "He's still a jerk!"

Katie realized Milton had been watching her. She smiled. "Don't be jealous."

"Jealous? I don't know what you're talking about."

Katie turned to greet the first visitors to their exhibit. The offer was made to teach the use of map and compass, but not taken.

"This is sure different from McKinley," Milton said, after many visitors had come and gone. "I mean, most people aren't even taking time to read our information. If I had known it was going to be like this, I would have suggested we figure out some sort of demonstration. Like Rudy and his stupid pieces of bark."

They both looked over to where Rudy had a sizable crowd around him.

"Rudy's a bit of a showman," Katie said.

"Yeah, but is it science?"

"The information Rudy has provided explains the scientific reasoning behind everything he's doing."

"You're assuming that someone's going to read it. I don't think anyone's taking the time to read anything today."

"Well, I am."

Milton and Katie turned to see a judge carefully examining their project and reading the information they provided.

"We can show you how to use a map and compass," Milton said.

"I'm afraid there's not enough time," she said. Her only other comment was, "Nice graphics," before she moved on to the next exhibit.

"Well, she didn't look very encouraging," Milton said.

"She's probably trying to appear impartial."

As it turned out, three more judges also assessed their project. None said very much, although each showed an interest. The judging took longer than anticipated. Noontime came and went without the participants being released to view the other exhibits.

"I'm starving," Milton said. "I'm going to go ahead and eat my lunch."

Milton and Katie ate their sack lunches while standing behind their exhibit. It wasn't until after one o'clock that the announcement was made that the judging phase of the science fair was over.

"It's about time!" Milton complained. "Do you want to go look around while I stay here and watch things?"

"Why don't you go first. Just give me a few minutes to use the restroom."

While Katie was gone, an announcement was made that the science fair, which was supposed to end at three o'clock, would continue until four in order to allow everyone a chance to see all the exhibits.

"I doubt Miss Droshky will want us to wait around until four," Katie said, returning.

"We'll have to if we want to be here when they award the prizes." Milton looked up at the clock. "I'll be back in forty-five minutes, which will leave you about the same amount of time to look around if Miss Droshky should shove us out of here at three."

As Milton began to walk through the hall, he soon realized why he and Katie had had so few takers for their hands-on activity. There were just too many exhibits to see. Some of the science projects were nothing short of amazing. Many students had used computers to design software programs that did everything from predict weather to design buildings. One student illustrated how bees saw flowers using an infrared detector she built herself. Another student had built a two-stage rocket and had a video showing its successful launch out in the desert. There was a converter designed to produce methane gas from corn stalks; a small engine modified to run on hydrogen produced by electrolysis; a demonstration on the use of fungi to clean sites contaminated by toxic wastes. Milton felt that, compared to these, his and Katie's project seemed like the work of kindergarteners. Of course, many of these ambitious projects reflected the greater resources, both human and material, available at large schools. It made Milton want to move back to the city, a desire he actually had not felt in several weeks.

It seemed that he had not gotten around to seeing even half of the exhibits before his forty-five minutes were up. He hurried back to find Katie talking to Miss Droshky.

"Good, you're back!" Miss Droshky said. "I was just telling Katie that I want us to leave as soon as the awards are handed out."

"But I haven't had time to see the other exhibits," Katie said.

"Well, hurry up. I want us to be out of here as soon as we can."

"I don't understand her," Katie said, after Miss Droshky had gone. "You'd think with her being a science teacher she'd encourage us to take in as much as possible, even if it means getting back late."

"Don't worry about her. Just go and enjoy the exhibits. There's some pretty amazing stuff."

Around two-thirty, the crowds began to thin and Milton thought it would not hurt to box up the topo maps, since they had only used them a few times. He put them in the small box they had been packed in and set the box on the floor under the table. The rest of their exhibit would only take a few minutes to pack. At three o'clock, Exploratorium volunteers began to circulate through the hall, distributing bright red folders. Some of the folders had prize ribbons attached. The folder that was placed on Milton and Katie's table did not. Though disappointed, Milton was not surprised.

The shadow of Miss Droshky fell over him as he opened up the folder. "Leave that for later, Milton. I want you to hurry and pack up things. Where's Katie?"

"I'm right here," Katie said, hurrying forward.

"Good! Help Milton pack. Let's see if we can beat the mob out of here."

"I see we didn't win a ribbon," Katie said, once Miss Droshky had moved on. "What's in the folder?"

"It looks to be some gift certificates and free admissions to other places like the Exploratorium."

"Well, that's a nice consolation."

"Do you think Rudy won a ribbon?"

"I took second place in the category of science medicine," Rudy said, suddenly appearing at their table.

"Well, you certainly deserved it," Katie said, "especially after the way you helped that lady."

"I wouldn't have won anything if it hadn't been for you guys." He turned to face Milton. "Mrs. Reese told me it was your idea I should come." He held out his hand to shake. "This has meant a lot to me, Milton. Thanks."

Milton took Rudy's hand, not knowing what to say. Rudy did not have any more words either. It seemed a tipping point in their relationship. It was Katie who gave them a shove in the right direction. "Milton, Rudy's got more stuff than we have, so why don't you help him carry his things to the van?"

Rudy did have a lot of stuff, and it took Milton and Rudy three trips to get it all in the van; three very wet trips, for it was raining. Their fellow students had already finished loading and were in their seats by the time they were done. Rudy climbed into the wide back seat and sat next to Anna Pease and Elizabeth Walters. Katie was already seated next to Rebecca Berkowitz in the middle row. That left Milton having to sit in the front with Miss Droshky.

"Has everyone got their seatbelt on?" Miss Droshky said.

"Yes, Miss Droshky," her passengers chorused.

"Wait!" Milton cried, unlatching his seatbelt. "I forgot my maps!"

"Leave them!" Miss Droshky ordered.

But Milton wasn't about to leave valuable topo maps that had cost so much of his savings. He ran back into the hall and found them where he had left them in a box under the table.

"Now may we leave?" Miss Droshky said upon Milton's return.

"Sorry, Miss Droshky," Milton said.

"I just hope we can miss the rush-hour traffic," she replied. She glanced at the clock on the dashboard. "As it is, it looks like we'll be an hour late getting back."

Milton was getting fed up with Miss Droshky's obsession with time. "What does it matter if we're a little late?"

Miss Droshky ignored Milton's question and concentrated upon getting out of the Exploratorium parking lot.

"I bet I know why Miss Droshky's in a hurry to get back," Rebecca Berkowitz said, leaning forward. "She doesn't want to miss *Love's Hospital.*"

A guilty look appeared on Miss Droshky's face.

"So, who's you're favorite character, Miss Droshky?" Rebecca said.

Miss Droshky cleared her throat before answering. "I'd have to go with Dr. Ramekins."

"Ugh! He's too old!"

Miss Droshky glanced at Rebecca in her rearview mirror. "Not to me, he's not."

"I'll take Dr. Love," Rebecca said. "He's gorgeous!"

Milton shook his head in disgust. All this rushing around just to not miss some stupid soap opera. Ignoring the discussion of Doctors Love and Ramekins, Milton got out his writing pad. A little water was trickling down the dashboard and onto the floor from a leaky seal in the windshield. Milton tucked his feet under him so they would not get wet and began to write.

Chapter 25

Ramblin' Red dreamt that he was wandering around in the desert on foot. He almost never traveled on foot, which begged the question of where was Cricket? Yet Ramblin' Red's immediate problem was that of a monumental thirst. He felt as if he had been walking for days with nothing to drink. Then he saw before him a curtain of rain descending from a mighty thunderhead. Though footsore and nearly dead from dehydration, Ramblin' Red ran forward, only to have the cloud evaporate just as he got under it. Furthermore, the thirsty ground had sucked up all the rain that had fallen. He fell to his knees and pressed his face to the earth, which, though cool upon his face, offered nothing to ease his suffering. Yet while kneeling he heard the unmistakable sound of a drop of water falling into a pool. He pushed himself up onto his feet, yet try as he might, he could not find the source of the sound.

Ramblin' Red woke from his dream to the sound of rain upon a tin roof. He opened his eyes and followed the path of a drop of water as it rolled down the metal's corrugation then fell with a "ping" into a rusty pail. The sound brought to mind his thirst. He tried to sit up, but his head spun so violently he was forced to lie back down. "Water!" he croaked. "Water!"

There was the sound of a chair scraping on the floor, followed by Nero Marceau's voice. "Doctor, come quick! He's awake!"

Dr. Laura Sutcliffe came running in from another room. To Ramblin' Red's eyes she looked as if she had not slept in days, which was pretty much the case. "Water please, Doctor."

Dr. Sutcliffe filled a glass from a bedside pitcher then helped hold his head as he gulped down the precious liquid. "Not too fast," she cautioned.

But Ramblin' Red could not drink fast enough. "More!" he demanded when the glass was empty.

"Not right now." She lowered his head onto the pillow. "You've had nothing in your stomach for days, and I don't want you vomiting what you just drank."

Ramblin' Red had no recollection of the time having passed. "You mean to tell me I've been loafing around in bed for days?"

"And in my bed, too!"

Ramblin' Red turned his head to see Randy Stark standing in the doorway. "I don't mean to cheat nobody out of his bed," he said, struggling to rise.

The three rushed to ease him back down.

"I was just joshing you, partner," Randy Stark said. "You're welcome to bunk down here as long you like." He motioned toward a room behind him from which good smells were emanating. "How you feeling? Could you use a bite to eat?"

Now that his thirst was somewhat abated, Ramblin' Red realized how hungry he was. "I could stand a bite or two. That is, if you got some to spare."

Randy Stark looked a bit sheepish. "Thanks to someone I know, I got plenty. How about a nice bowl of beef stew?"

"Just the broth," Dr. Sutcliffe said, following Stark out of the room. "I don't want to tax his digestive system at this stage in his recovery."

Nero dragged a chair closer to the bed and sat down. "Those two have been like two mother hens watching over you," he said.

"How did I end up here?"

"Sheriff Roswell hauled you here in Stark's buckboard. It was the closest place we could take you."

"Sounds like I owe a bunch of people a heap of thanks."

"Not in the least, Nero Marceau," Dr. Sutcliffe said, returning with a tray.

Nero shook his head. "About all I did was give Jupiter a little exercise."

Dr. Sutcliffe set the tray on an empty keg that served as a bedside table. "Nero raced to town to get the medicines I needed. If it had been a horse less swift or rider less determined, you would not have–" She turned away so they would not see the tears that suddenly came to her eyes.

"I may have done my little part," Nero said, "but it's the doctor here that you owe your life to. She's a tremendously gifted physician."

Ramblin' Red was overwhelmed with gratitude. "I can't thank you all enough."

"Well, you can thank me by making sure you get well," Nero said. "It seems a couple of gentlemen were foolish enough to bet me that you weren't going to make it." He pushed back his chair and stood up. "Speaking of betting, I confess an urge to get a deck of cards in my hands, so if I'm not needed for the present, I'll return to town."

Ramblin' Red held out his hand. "Thanks for all you done, Nero."

Nero shook hands. "I'll be back in a couple of days to see how my investment is doing."

"That Nero sure likes to play the devil," Ramblin' Red said, once Nero had departed, "but I suspect there's more goodness in him than he'd like to admit."

"I don't know what I would've done without him," Dr. Sutcliffe replied. "Did you know he served in the medical corps during the war?"

"There's a whole lot about Nero that's a mystery."

"Like someone else I know," she said, dipping a spoon into a bowl of beef broth. "Now, let's see how much of this we can get down you."

Ramblin' Red had not been spoon fed since infancy. Yet he was in no condition to raise an objection; just shaking hands with Nero had left him exhausted. Halfway through his feeding, he fell asleep, and once again he dreamt, only this time his dream was as pleasant as his last had been distressing. He was standing in a field of corn, looking back toward a white clapboard house that stood like a sailing ship in a sea of green. In the past, he had always steered clear of farms and the toil they represented, yet now he was filled with a great contentment as he surveyed the rows of lush, ripening corn. His musing was interrupted by the slamming of a screen door, and he turned to see the figure of Laura Sutcliffe, medical bag in hand, descending porch steps.

She met him halfway down a row of corn. "I'm going to see how Mrs. Cather and her new baby are faring. I should be back in time to fix us lunch." She set down her bag and pinned up a stray lock of hair.

"That will just give me time to weed the vegetable patch," Ramblin' Red said.

She moved closer, took his hand, and they both gazed across the acres of fertile land. They did not need words to express that what they saw was good.

When Ramblin Red woke, he again tried to sit up, and this time he succeeded in planting his feet upon the floor. All he was wearing was his long johns. He saw that someone had laundered his other clothes and laid them neatly folded upon a nearby chair. But as he stood to retrieve his clothes, the room began to spin, and he was forced to lean upon the bedpost to keep from toppling over.

"And just what do you think you're doing?" Dr. Sutcliffe cried, entering the room.

Still holding onto the bedpost, Ramblin Red sat down upon the bed. "Trying to get dressed, and doing a pretty poor job of it."

"You'll do no such thing!" she exclaimed, pulling back the bed covers and motioning for him to get back under them.

"But what about Kid Torkasky?"

"What about him?"

"Is he still loose? If so, somebody's got to go after him."

"Well, that somebody is certainly not going to be you!" When Ramblin' Red did not show any sign of returning to bed, she tried to reason with him. "The sheriff organized a posse, and right now they're in pursuit of that horrid criminal."

Ramblin' Red shook his head and wished he had not, for the room spun. "You don't understand, the sheriff can't shoot worth a hoot."

"Well, Randy Stark sure can, and he's gone to join the posse."

Ramblin' Red continued to stare at his clothes on the chair.

Dr. Sutcliffe laid a hand upon Ramblin' Red's arm. "Please, Max, I almost lost you once. Don't put me through that again."

With a sigh, Ramblin' Red relinquished the bed post and lay back down. As Dr. Sutcliffe drew the covers over him, he saw that her hair was tucked up as it had been in his dream.

"Do you always wear your hair up like that?"

Dr. Sutcliffe touched her hair. "Well, yes. They taught us in medical school that a doctor must always convey authority. When I wear my hair up like this it means, 'I'm the doctor, and you're going to do what I say.'" She wagged a finger at him. "So, you're going to do what I say, Max Schaefer, and stay in bed until you get well."

Ramblin' Red smiled. "Yes, ma'am."

"Good! Now, is there anything else I can get you?"

He did not reply, but studied her face.

"What is it, Max?"

He cleared his throat. "I had a dream about you," he said. "About us."

Her eyes brightened. "Did you?"

"Yes," he said, but did not elaborate. He felt the time not right to tell her of his dream. Neither was it time to ask her the question he wanted to ask, for he feared that, at this point in time, any answer she might give would be unduly influenced by an obligation she might feel toward him. There would be time enough to pose his question when he was well and able. On top of that, there was the unfinished business with Kid Torkasky. "Stark went with them, you said?"

"Yes," she replied.

"Then I suspect they'll catch the Kid."

But what neither of them knew was that while Sheriff Roswell and his posse were out chasing after Kid Torkasky, the Kid had joined up with a couple of his old henchmen, and they were making plans to rob the Stockmans Bank of Pandemonium.

Chapter 26

Milton looked up from his writing pad, and saw that they had left the city and were now headed back up into the mountains. The rain had not abated, and the drip from the broken seal in the window was soaking the floor mat.

"You know, Milton, you aren't the only person who writes," Miss Droshky said, as she stared out at the road.

Milton had never heard Miss Droshky call his writing anything other than "scribbling." "You're a writer, Miss Droshky?"

Miss Droshky did not reply, but concentrated upon driving.

"What kind of things do you write?"

"If I told you, you'd laugh."

"No, I won't. Promise." He crossed his heart.

Miss Droshky looked at him then back at the road. "I write romances."

Milton had to bite his cheeks to keep from laughing. All this did was send his laughter up his nose.

"You can laugh all you want," Miss Droshky said, "but I'll have you know that romances are the most popular form of fiction on the market today."

Yeah, Milton thought, and likely cow manure is the most popular form of fertilizer. Yet why should he surprised that Miss Droshky should write romances, having seen her read so many?

"I'll have you know, Mr. Smarty Pants," Miss Droshky continued, "that I have a literary agent, so put that in your pipe and smoke it."

"I don't smoke," Milton said.

"You know what I mean." Miss Droshky flicked on her turn signal. "This is that short cut I've been looking for."

"Why are we going this way?" Rudy said as the van turned sharply.

Miss Droshky glanced at Rudy in her review mirror. "Because it's a short cut. It'll save us at least forty-five minutes going this way."

"But this is an old logging road. It's not even paved all the way."

"Relax, Rudy," Miss Droshky said, "I've been this way lots of times."

Milton recalled something Mr. Cunningham had told him. "Don't they close these roads as soon as it starts snowing?"

"Does it look like it's snowing?" Miss Droshky said, pointing at the windshield. And no sooner had she said this than the rain turned to large flakes of snow. "It doesn't matter. We'll be back on the main road by the time there's any accumulation."

Milton picked up his box of maps and started looking through them.

"You and your maps," Miss Droshky said.

"I just want to see where we are." He had to study a few maps before finding the one that showed the road they were on. The old logging road was indeed an alternate route, shorter than the main highway, though much windier. The map indicated it was paved at both ends with a section of about eight miles of gravel in between. "According to this, there's a pass we have to cross that's about six thousand feet in elevation."

"I know the road, Milton."

Milton did a quick calculation. The road started at around four thousand feet, which meant they would have to climb two thousand feet before getting to the pass. On average, for every thousand feet of elevation gained, the temperature dropped three and one-half degrees Fahrenheit, which meant at the top of the pass it would be seven degrees colder. Consequently, it could have been snowing up there already. Milton folded his map and put it back in the box. "I guess if the road becomes impassable, we can just turn around and go back down. Of course, that means we'll get back even later."

"We're not getting back any later than we have to." The weather appeared to affirm Miss Droshky's decision, for the road stayed clear, and the section of gravel, when they reached it, was well graded, and they made good time.

"We're nearing the pass," Miss Droshky said, "and look how good this road is. It's straight as an arrow."

True, Milton thought, but most of it had been so winding, he was surprised they weren't all car sick. He was about to voice this when something large moved at the edge of his vision.

"Miss Droshky, look out!" Katie yelled.

A large buck with a huge set of antlers had stepped out onto the road. Miss Droshky swerved to the right to miss it. But the buck panicked and ran directly into the path of the van, forcing Miss Droshky to turn further right. The wheels skidded on the soft shoulder. Miss Droshky turned into the direction of the skid, but they were going too fast, and the van went over the embankment.

"Oh, God!" Miss Droshky yelled, as the van careened down the mountain side.

Milton felt his heart in his throat. "Brake!" he yelled. "Brake!"

"I am braking!"

There was a sharp drop-off, and the van flew over it. As the van hurled through the air, it snapped off sapling pines as if they were matchsticks. Branches rattled against the undercarriage and hammered against the doors and windows. There was the sound of breaking glass and the clamor of everyone screaming.

The van came back to earth with an ear-piercing screech of tortured steel.

"Miss Droshky! Miss Droshky!" Milton yelled, pointing through the cracked windshield. The van was hurling toward a massive ponderosa pine. "Turn! Turn!"

But Miss Droshky, slumped over the steering wheel, was incapable of responding. Milton grabbed the steering wheel, but it was too late. The van smashed into the pine with an impact that lifted the back wheels off the ground. Anything not belted down came flying forward, and Milton found himself sandwiched between an exploding air bag and his seat, which had slid forward upon impact. Steam rolled through the van from the smashed radiator. And all the while everyone was screaming.

Then the screaming stopped and there was silence, save for the hissing of steam. The silence lasted for about minute before someone started to cry. Milton wondered if that someone was himself. He felt as if had been hit over the head with a baseball bat. Nothing made sense. It seemed someone was shouting something about a tree.

Then everything became clear. He was pinned against the dashboard of the van. His teacher was unconscious. Someone was crying. It was snowing. It was dark. They were perched on the side of a mountain, miles from anywhere, and no one, absolutely no one, knew where they were.

Well, partner, said the voice of Ramblin' Red in Milton's head. *You asked for an adventure, and you sure got one!*

Chapter 27

Rudy was the first one to move. He slid open the side door, which, miraculously, still functioned.

"Is everyone all right?" he said, standing on the ground, looking back into the van. No one answered. "Someone answer me!" he yelled. "Elizabeth, are you okay?"

"My arm hurts!"

"At least you're talking. Anna, how about you?"

Anna was the one crying.

Katie turned around and studied Anna by the overhead light. "I think she's okay." She turned to Rebecca slumped in the seat beside her. "You okay, Rebecca?"

Rebecca, sitting up, brushed away tears. "I thought we were all going to die."

"Milton, what about you?" Katie said.

Milton did not answer.

"Milton!"

"I can't move my legs."

"Oh, no!"

"I mean, I'm pinned. Can someone pull my seat back?"

That required clearing out the debris composed of scattered science fair projects. Rudy opened the passenger door and began to sweep the stuff out onto the snow. "I think I smell leaking gas," he said.

Someone screamed.

"Don't panic!" Rudy shouted. "Everyone get out of the van and move away from it.”

“But it's dark out there!” Elizabeth cried.

“All right, hold on.” Rudy ran around to the rear of the van, swung open the rear door, and began to rummage around until he found the flashlight that had been part of his wilderness survival exhibit. “Okay, I want everyone who can to follow me.” He led them down the slope away from the van.

Katie stayed behind, trying to pull Milton's seat back. Rudy returned and working together they were able to retract the seat far enough so that Milton could climb out of the van.

“You okay?” Rudy said.

“Yeah, but I think Miss Droshky is hurt bad.”

Rudy shined his flashlight on Miss Droshky. Katie gasped. Miss Droshky, slumped over the steering wheel, was bleeding from a cut on her head.

“She must've hit her head on the steering wheel or something,” Rudy said.

“I think a tree branch smashed through her window,” Milton said.

“What are we going to do?” Katie said.

“Okay, let's think,” Rudy said, tapping the flashlight against the palm of his hand. “The first thing is to always assess the situation.”

“Well, that's not hard,” Milton said. “We're screwed!”

“Shut up!” Rudy barked. “At least no one is seriously injured.”

“Except Miss Droshky,” Katie said.

“Right,” Rudy said. “So, let's see how bad she is.”

The three made their way to the driver's side of the van, which was not easy; the sloping ground was slick with snow, and small bits of shale turned under their feet. Rudy got to the driver's side door first and opened it. Reaching in, he felt for Miss Droshky's pulse.

“Why you doing that?” Milton said. “You can see she's breathing.”

“Milton, will you shut up!” Rudy said.

“You're not helping, Milton,” Katie said.

“I'm trying to see how strong her pulse is,” Rudy said. “It seems a little slow." He passed the light of the flashlight over Miss Droshky's body. "I think it's just her head that's hurt. I won't be able to know for sure until we get her out of the van."

"Shouldn't we just leave her where she is?" Katie said.

"We can't," Rudy replied. "The smell of gas is really strong in here."

"Okay," Milton said, "so, how are we going to move her, and where are we going to move her to?"

Rudy used his flashlight to survey the area around them. "There's a flat spot under that pine tree over there. We can set Miss Droshky under the branches, which will help keep the snow off of her. Milton, you and I are going to use a two-man carry."

"I don't think I can lift her."

"I can help," Katie said.

"No," Rudy said. "I need for you to help stabilize her head. We don't know if she has a neck injury. Go around to the other side of the van, and when we start to lift Miss Droshky, you support her head."

While Katie went around the van, Rudy quickly showed Milton how to clasp arms to form a two-man carry.

"I still don't think I can lift her," Milton said.

"I don't know if I can either, but we've got to try!"

It wasn't a picture-perfect carry, but the three managed to get Miss Droshky out of the van and over to the tree, doing more dragging than lifting.

"I'll see if I can find something to put under her," Katie said.

"What are we going to do now?" Milton said. He had already assumed Rudy to be the leader.

Rudy shook his head. "You're right, Milton, we're screwed. I mean, look at us. We're out in the middle of nowhere, in the dark, in a snowstorm, and no one even knows we're here."

"Maybe someone will drive by and see us."

Rudy looked up the slope to the road, which was about two hundred feet above them. "I doubt anyone will be coming this way. Miss Droshky was nuts to take this road. I don't know what we're going to do."

Katie returned with two lightweight jackets. "These were all I could find to put under her."

Rudy shook his head. "We're going to need to wear those. It's freezing."

"I don't think any of us brought warm jackets," Katie said.

"None of us were expecting this," Milton said.

"So what are we going to do?" Katie said.

"We need to find my survival gear," Rudy said. "There's stuff we can use. But first, we've got to see if there are any more flashlights."

They found two, one in the van's glove compartment and another clipped to the side panel under the dashboard on the driver's side.

Rudy handed Katie the bigger flashlight. "Take the two jackets and give them to whoever they belong to."

Milton pulled a jacket from the debris. "Katie wait! Here's another jacket."

"That's mine," she said, and stopped to put it on.

Rudy began to rummage through the wreckage. "Here's my emergency tent and some matches."

"There's a lot of paper we could use for a fire."

"Paper won't burn very long, but we might be able to gather some wood."

Milton found the lightweight jacket he had brought and put it on. He found his box of maps wedged between the two front seats. He hated to think he might have to burn all his lovely maps.

"Milton, what are you doing? If you're looking for a cell phone, forget it. There's no way we can get reception out here."

"I'm looking for the map that shows where we are."

"For Pete's sake, Milton! Forget the maps. Help me find my survival gear."

"Here it is!" He pocketed the map.

Katie returned along with Rebecca.

"My cell phone doesn't work here," Rebecca said.

"Surprise, surprise," Rudy said. "Look, you two, help find stuff that might be useful while I go set up the emergency tent."

"Will we all be able to fit inside it?" Rebecca said.

"It's only big enough for one person. We'll put Miss Droshky in it. She needs it the most."

Milton wanted to find his backpack. He had been thinking about Ramblin' Red and what he might have done in this situation. He had an idea. "Has anyone seen my backpack?"

"I think Rudy tossed it out," Rebecca said.

"Oh, great!" Everything that had been thrown out was now blanketed in snow. He began to dig through the snow. By the time he found his backpack, his fingers were so cold, he was barely able to move the zipper.

"What's so important about your backpack?" Rebecca said.

"It has my compasses. I think I may have an idea for getting help."

"What is it?"

Hearing the excitement in her voice, Milton wished he had not said anything. "I won't know if it's even possible until I can climb up to the road."

"I think we should stay together," Katie said.

"Me, too," Rebecca said.

"Look," Milton said, "I've got a hunch we may be only two, maybe three, miles from the main highway."

"How do you know?" Rebecca said.

"Yeah," Katie said, "you don't even know where we are."

"That's why I've got to get up to the road, so I can figure it out."

"Well, if you're going up there, I'm going with you," Katie said.

"Don't leave us!" Rebecca pleaded.

"It's all right, Rebecca," Katie said. "We won't be gone long." She turned to Milton. "Will we?"

Milton did not answer; he was thinking of something else. *I'm not like you Ramblin' Red. Can I really do what I'm thinking of doing?*

Chapter 28

The steep slope would have been hard to scramble up under the best of circumstances let alone slick with snow. The effort of climbing, however, warmed Milton and Katie, and by the time they reached the road, both were sweating.

"Okay," Milton said, struggling to get his breath. "I think I can figure out where we are."

"How?" Katie said. "We can't see anything to triangulate off of."

"We don't need to." He took his map from his back pocket and opened it up. "Shine the flashlight on the map." He ran his finger along the line that indicated the road. "Just before we went off road, we were at the beginning of a long straightaway. I'm pretty sure it's this one here."

"How can you be sure?" Katie said, pointing to another straight section of road on the map.

"Because this is the only section that's heading in the direction of thirty-two degrees north-northeast."

"I get it," Katie said. "If the compass shows the road going thirty-two degrees north-northeast…"

"Then we're on this section of the road." He took a compass out of his back pack. "There, I've put Red in the shed, so north is that way. Which means…" He sighted across the compass straight down the road. "Looks to me like this road is headed thirty-two degrees north-northeast."

Katie took the compass and repeated the procedure. "Okay, we know the section of road we're on, but it's a long straightaway; we could be anywhere along it."

Milton returned to the map. "I remember just before we went off the road we passed over a creek. The map shows it, so that puts us right about here. And look…" He ran his finger north across the map. "…the main highway takes a jag toward us. I figure it's about three miles from here—four tops."

"Milton, you can't be thinking about us going cross country to the highway!"

"Why not? We've done it before."

"But that was during the day, when it was sunny and warm. Now it's dark, and it's snowing."

"We can do like we did before, point-to-point navigation with one person going forward to establish a bearing."

"But that takes forever. And what if we're wrong? Look at the map; the main highway dips toward us only at this one point. If our bearing is off even by a little, we'll miss the highway altogether."

Milton rubbed his arms. He was cold again. "So, what are our alternatives, Katie?"

"We wait until someone comes to find us."

"And how long will that take? How long can we last up here? No one's brought any warm clothing. I think we should at least try to get help. It's what…"

"What?" Katie said.

He caught himself about to say it was what Ramblin' Red would do. "Oh, nothing."

"I think we need to talk this over with the others," Katie said.

They found the others huddled around a small fire made using scraps of paper, notebooks, and a little wood.

Rudy immediately confronted Milton. "You shouldn't have gone off like that. We've got to stay together."

"I think I know how we can get help."

"Rebecca said something about finding the main highway. Our best option is to stay put and wait until help arrives."

"But what if help doesn't arrive, or doesn't arrive soon enough? Miss Droshky needs medical attention right now. And how long can the rest of us last out here without warm clothing?"

"As long as we have to!" Rudy said.

Anna spoke up. "We're not all like you, Rudy. You're tough. I'm not used to this, and I'm really, really cold. At least let's hear Milton's idea."

Milton explained about the highway being only three to four miles away. "Using the compass and flashlights, two of us can go cross country from here to the highway."

"That's your plan?" Rudy said. "Wandering around in the dark, hoping you'll find the highway? Then what? What if you do find the highway and no one is out driving around in the middle of the night in the snow?"

"We won't be just wandering around," Katie said. "We'll be navigating point to point."

"Don't tell me you're planning to join Milton in this nutty plan?" Rudy said.

"Milton and I have done this before."

"And once we reach the highway," Milton said, "Someone's bound to come along eventually."

Rudy shook his head. "I still say our best bet is to sit tight and wait until help arrives. The survival guides all agree that that's the best plan."

"Milton," Elizabeth said, "it sounds like what you're planning to do is really risky."

"I wouldn't have brought this up if I didn't think we could do it." Yet having said this, he wondered if he was not biting off more than he could chew.

"Maybe we should take a vote," Rebecca said. "All in favor of Milton and Katie going for help, raise your hand."

Everyone raised their hand except Rudy.

"You two have no idea what you're getting into," he said. "I mean, just look at your shoes." He pointed to Milton's sneakers. "In no time your feet are going to be soaked. Then they will freeze, and you won't be able to walk."

Milton had not thought of that.

"Here," Rudy said, handing both Milton and Katie plastic grocery bags. "I gathered a bunch of these. Put them over your socks. That way your feet will stand a chance of staying dry."

"Thanks, Rudy," Milton said. "Any other advice?"

"Yeah, stay put!"

Milton began to take off his shoes and put the bags over his socks. "I'm not sure how long it will take us, but we'll go as quickly as we can."

"Wish us luck," Katie said.

"Luck," the group answered, though not with great enthusiasm.

"You're going to need more than luck," Rudy said. He handed Katie his flashlight. "Take this and don't let Buttock get lost."

Chapter 29

Milton and Katie once again stood on the road. "Okay," Milton said, looking at his watch, "it's just a little past six. Now we need to find the creek. That way we'll know exactly where we are."

They began to walk back down the road, shining their flashlights to each side.

"There it is!" Katie exclaimed.

"Good! Now according to the map, the main highway is seven degrees west of north." He studied his compass. "Which means it's that way." He used his flashlight as a pointer.

"Oh, Milton, we can hardly see anything."

It was true. The light did not penetrate the darkness very far on account of the falling snow, which meant they only would be able to navigate from point to point in short stretches.

"It's going to take us hours and hours to get to the highway," Katie said.

"Maybe. But how long will it take for someone to find us if we just sit and do nothing? It could be days."

From behind them came the sound of footsteps crunching on the snow. They both swung their flashlights around.

"Not in my eyes!" Rudy yelled. "You're blinding me." Rudy had on his backpack and a climbing rope was looped over his neck and shoulder.

"What are you doing?" Katie said.

"And why the rope?" Milton said.

"I'm gonna make sure you two idiots don't freeze to death before you find the road. As for the rope, I believe in being prepared. You never know when a bit of rope might come in handy."

"You're going with us?" Milton said.

"I've got nothing else better to do."

"What about the others?" Katie said.

"They're all huddled together in the van. It's warmer in there than over that dinky fire."

"You're not worried about the gas leak?"

"If the van hasn't caught fire yet, it's not going to." He looked down at the creek. "So, which way is the highway?"

Milton pointed with his flashlight. "It's that way."

"Only the light doesn't shine very far because it's snowing," Katie said.

"Tell you what," Rudy said, "I've always had a good sense of direction. I'll walk that way and you direct me left or right."

Katie handed Rudy her flashlight.

"Wait!" Milton said. "I just had an idea." He took from his backpack a sheet of paper and a pencil. "Keep a tally of the number of paces you take. That way we'll have some idea of how far we've gone." He folded the paper into quarters then handed it to Rudy along with the pencil.

Rudy had not walked more than ten paces when Milton stopped him again. "Now what?" Rudy said.

"Your backpack has reflectors on it."

"Yeah, so what?"

"So, it's perfect. I can see to guide you."

"What should I to do?" Katie said.

"Here," Milton said, turning his back to Katie. "Get the other compass out of my pack. With both of us taking bearings, there'll be less chance of making a mistake."

Because of the reflectors, Rudy could go a long way and still be seen. "Okay, that's far enough!" Milton yelled. "Go a little to the right. Stop! Now don't move until we get to you." The ground was fairly level with little to trip them up. Only the snow slowed them.

"Did you write down the number of paces?" Milton said to Rudy.

"Yeah. Now, which way?"

Milton and Katie studied their compasses. "That way," they said in unison.

Rudy did not lie when he said he had a good sense of direction. He was able to keep on course even when he had to detour around a tree or another object.

"I'm glad Rudy decided to come with us," Katie said.

Milton had to admit he was glad too. "He's really comfortable in the woods. I guess that comes from spending so much time out of doors with his dad."

Rudy suddenly stopped. "What's the matter?" Milton yelled.

"Come here!" he yelled.

"I hope he hasn't run into a cliff or something," Katie said.

"The map shows very few topo lines between here and the road," Milton said. He stumbled over a tree branch hidden by the snow and went down on one knee.

Katie waited while Milton dusted off his pants then they both hurried forward. "What's the matter?" Milton said.

"Nothing much," Rudy said. "It's just that the ground slopes off pretty steeply, and I didn't think you'd be able to see me if I went past this point."

"So, how many paces have you gone?"

"Is it so important that I count my steps? I could go faster if I didn't have to think about them."

"But we need some way of gauging how far we've come," Milton said.

Rudy shook his head. "No, what we need is to get to the road as fast as we can."

"No, what we need—"

"Listen, you two," Katie interrupted. "We'll never get anywhere if you start fighting. Besides, I've got an idea. I'll count the paces. It'll help me keep my mind off how cold it is."

Rudy handed Katie the paper and pencil. "Okay, which way, now?"

Milton pointed and Rudy trudged off.

"Milton," Katie said, as she doubled checked the bearing, "we didn't check to see if Rudy was lined up correctly on that last section."

Milton groaned. "I was so anxious about why he stopped, I forgot. Maybe we'd better go back."

"I don't think he was far off our bearing."

"He better not have been, or we'll miss the highway."

"Okay!" Rudy yelled back. "How am I doing?"

"Go left!" Milton shouted. "Stop!"

Once settled into a routine, they moved across country with surprising speed, considering the conditions. They came to a creek and had difficultly crossing because the rocks they used as stepping stones were icy slick. Still, they managed to get across without anyone getting their feet wet.

"Let's stop a second," Milton said. "I want to check the map."

"Is this the same creek as the one where we started?" Rudy said.

Milton shook his head. "It's a different one." He pointed to the map as Rudy looked over his shoulder. "We're right here, which means we're about a quarter of the way to the highway." Milton turned to Katie who stood apart. "Katie, don't you want to look at the map?"

"I'm so cold," she murmured.

Milton's heart sank. He did not know what he could do for her.

Rudy took charge. "All right, you two, calisthenics!" He set down his rope. "We'll start with jumping jacks."

Milton joined Rudy in jumping jacks, but Katie barely went through the motions. "Come on, Katie." Rudy barked. "Get your butt in gear!" He stood over her like a drill sergeant, forcing her into activity by the power of his presence. "Now, run in place, and don't stop until I tell you."

Both Katie and Milton ran until they were gasping for air. "I've got to stop," Milton said. "The air's so cold, it hurts my lungs."

"Okay," Rudy said, "but from now on, we're going to stop every fifteen minutes and do calisthenics."

No one offered any objections.

"Which way now?" Rudy said.

Milton and Katie pointed.

Rudy's flashlight made a circle of light that got smaller and smaller the farther he went. Suddenly he changed directions.

"What's Rudy doing?" Milton said. "He's going way off our course."

"He must be having to go around some fallen trees."

The light from Rudy's flashlight disappeared altogether.

"Rudy, come back!" Milton yelled. But Rudy did not come back. "Why won't that jerk listen to me?"

"I think we should trust him," Katie said.

But Milton was uncertain he *could* trust him. Despite the improved relationship between them, Milton still thought of Rudy as a jock, and to Milton that meant a tendency to act without thinking. Milton had to admit his own fault was a stubbornness when it came to doing things his own way.

"Maybe one of us should go after him," Katie said.

Before Milton could answer, the light from Rudy's flashlight reappeared. "Okay," Rudy yelled, "how am I doing?"

"Go left." Milton yelled back. "A little more. Stop! Here we come!"

It wasn't fallen trees that had forced Rudy to veer off course, but a large granite outcropping with snow piled knee deep on the windward side. When they caught up to Rudy, they found him emptying his shoes of snow.

"My toes are so cold, they hurt," Katie said, sitting on a rock and rubbing a foot through her shoe.

"Here, let me," Rudy said. He quickly unlaced Katie's shoe

"Ow!" she cried, as Rudy began to rub. "That hurts!"

"It'll will only hurt for a little while, until your foot warms up."

"Your hands are warm."

"That's because I'm warm blooded. I'm hardly cold at all."

"I wish I were that way."

Milton was worried about the time they were losing. "I think we should hurry up and get going."

"Not before I warm Katie's feet," Rudy said, tying back on her shoe then removing her other one. "If necessary, I'll stop and make a fire."

"With what?" Milton said. "All the wood is wet from the snow."

Rudy did not reply, but finished with Katie's other foot.

"Rudy's right," Katie said, as they once more watched Rudy break trail. "It won't do anybody any good if we freeze to death before we can get help."

"I know," Milton said. "It's just…" It was just that he was worried, but he did not want to admit it. This was not one of his Ramblin' Red stories where he could make everything come out all right. What if instead of leading them to the highway, he was leading them to their deaths? "Lately, I'd been thinking how it'd be fun to have some adventure in my life." He shook his head. "What was I thinking?" He reached out and touched Katie on her sleeve. "I'm glad you're with me, Katie."

"Really? I feel useless, like I'm a weight slowing you two down."

"Not true! Without you, Rudy and I would be at each other's throats. And two navigators are better than one, especially under these conditions."

"Thanks for saying that. Now I feel like we're going to make it."

"Of course, we are!" He said, trying to sound confident, but a little voice in his head, was asking, "Are we?"

Chapter 30

"Okay!" Rudy yelled back. "Which way now?"

Milton looked at his compass. "Go a little right! Stop!"

Katie, consulting her compass, shook her head. "Did you have Red in the shed?"

Milton checked his bearing again. "No, I messed up!" It was because his hands were shaking from the cold. He forced himself to hold the compass steady. "Rudy!" he yelled. "Go back to the left. Farther! Stop there!"

"You didn't just do that to make me feel useful, did you?" Katie said.

"No way!" He tucked his hands under his arms, trying to warm them. He was afraid he would no longer to be able to read the compass if he could not keep his hands from shaking.

Somewhere Milton had read that fear required energy, and people sometimes stopped being afraid, not because there was nothing to be afraid of, but because they were just too tired to be fearful. Cold, as well as fatigue, also affected one's ability to sense fear, dulling the mind as well as slowing reaction times.

Whether from cold or fatigue, Milton reached a point where he was no longer afraid, though the absence of fear should have been a warning, a reason itself to fear. He wondered if it was the same for Katie, but was too tired to ask. He knew she was moving slower. In fact, they were all moving slower because the snow was getting deeper. He also knew that Katie had given up keeping a record of the number of steps they had come.

He looked at his watch. They had left the others well over three hours ago. He tried to translate time into distance. On a good trail, on a nice day, a hiker could travel up to three miles an hour. But they were not on a good trail, and it was certainly not a nice day. His original estimation of distance was based on the grids shown on the topo map, scaled at one mile apart. But that was one mile as the crow flies, not as the tired human walks.

"How's everybody doing?" Rudy said when Milton and Katie came up to him.

"Okay," Milton lied. He knew he was not doing very well at all.

"Katie?"

Katie could not answer because of her chattering teeth.

"That does it!" Rudy said. "I'm building a fire."

"With what wood?" Milton said.

"With this wood!" Rudy reached up and snapped a dead branch off a tree. "And this!" He snapped off another branch.

Milton helped him, and soon each had a small armload of wood. Rudy swept a section of ground clear using a large stick. Then he pulled out of his pocket something that looked like a lump of melted wax.

"What's that?" Milton said.

"It's pitch." Rudy said. "I pulled it off a tree earlier. Pitch really burns fast and hot."

It was true. Rudy held a lighted match to the lump of pitch, and it immediately caught fire and burned with an intense heat. They piled dead branches over it and soon had a fire going.

"Oh, that feels good," Katie said, putting her hands above the flames.

It was more than good, Milton thought. It was life-saving. As the warmth began to travel through him he began to think more clearly. "I think we should've come to the highway by now."

"I've been thinking the same thing for quite a while," Katie said.

"So what happened?" Rudy said, "Are we lost?"

Milton got out his map, careful not to hold it too near the flames. "I just wish there were some landmarks, but everything around here is pretty much the same, just lots of trees."

"At least we're not having to scramble up mountains," Katie said.

Rudy looked over Milton's shoulder. "So where do you think we are?"

Milton was not sure exactly. Since the highway took a jag in their direction before reversing direction, they could have passed to one side of it without seeing it. "I wish it were daytime or not snowing, anything to make it likely that someone would be out driving. Then we could either see or hear a car."

"We could wait it out until morning," Rudy said. "Keep the fire going. Maybe construct some kind of shelter to keep the snow off of us. I'm sure I could build something."

Milton had to admit this was a good idea. He again looked at his watch. It would take at least nine hours before it would be light enough to see. Could his classmates hold out for another nine hours? Could Miss Droshky?

"We told the others we would get help," Milton said. He began to fold up his map. "I think we should continue to try to find the highway."

"You're the boss," Rudy said.

Was Rudy being sarcastic? It would be just like him. "You're as much a boss as I am."

"We're a team," Katie said. "As a team, we should all be in agreement."

Rudy nodded. "Okay. I vote that we keep looking for the highway."

"But not for too much longer," Katie said. "Because if we are lost…"

"Then we'll just get more lost," Rudy said.

Milton again looked at his watch. "Why don't we continue on for another half-hour? If we don't find the highway by then, we'll wait until morning."

"Will we be able to build another fire?" Katie said.

Rudy pulled from his pocket another lump of pitch. "They're not hard to find, if you know where to look." He stood up, put on his backpack. "Okay, which way?"

Both Milton and Katie consulted their compasses then pointed.

Rudy looped his rope over one shoulder and started off.

"I don't know what I would've done had Rudy not built this fire," Katie said.

Milton had to agree. This whole venture had given him a respect for Rudy and his way of doing things. He just wondered whether Rudy might now feel differently toward him. That would likely depend on whether they actually found the highway.

"Rudy's sure going a long way," Katie said. "I can barely see his light."

"It could be the batteries are getting low." He had begun to notice this problem with his.

The light from Rudy's flashlight suddenly disappeared altogether. They waited, but it did not reappear.

"Maybe he dropped his flashlight and can't find it," Katie said.

"Rudy!" they yelled.

Silence.

"Rudy!"

No reply. It seemed that Rudy had fallen off the edge of the earth.

Chapter 31

One moment Rudy had been breaking trail over a flat section of ground, the next he was falling through the air. It was like he dropped into a hole with no bottom. He landed hard but continued to plummet like a toboggan racing down a mountain. He raked his side on a rock, but the pain did not register in his panic. Try as he might, he could not arrest his fall, for there was nothing to grip but snow, which slipped through his fingers as if it were white flour. He crashed through a bush, tearing a pant leg. The branch he grabbed broke off. A second branch proved sturdier. Then he was dangling by one arm with nothing under his feet. A pain like a knife between his ribs prevented him from raising his other arm. He was tempted to let go, to slide further down the mountainside with the hope of finding a place to plant his feet. If only he had not lost his flashlight in his fall. There was nothing but darkness and the sound of rushing water coming from somewhere far below him.

When Milton and Katie came to the end of Rudy's tracks, they found only a hole in a drift of snow.

"Rudy! Rudy!" they yelled.

No answer.

Inching his way forward, Milton shone the flashlight down the hole.

"What do you see?" Katie said.

"It just goes almost straight down."

"Oh, no!"

Something that looked like a tree root stuck out of the snow a little way down the hole. Lying on his stomach, Milton tried to reach down and grab it.

"What are you doing?" Katie said.

"I think I see Rudy's rope, only I can't quite reach it."

"Be careful!"

He stretched out farther and managed to pinch the rope between his middle and index fingers. Small tugs succeeding in freeing enough rope so he could get a good grip on it. It was stiff from having been buried in the snow, and so icy, it stung his hands as he gathered it in.

Rudy had heard his name being called, but he could hardly breathe with the pain in his side, let alone cry out. All he could do was cling to his branch with one hand and pray that Milton and Katie would come to his rescue. Help could not come too soon; his hand was going numb, and he did not know how much longer he could hold on.

Milton was thinking he could tie off the rope then throw it down the hole so that Rudy could have something to pull himself up with. He looked for something to tie the rope to. "What happened to all the stupid trees?" For a space of forty or fifty feet around them there was not so much as a twig sticking out of the snow. Milton turned in a circle, shining the flashlight. There was something unnatural about this clearing; the snow lay too flat and even, as if some giant had smoothed it out with the side of his hand.

"Here, take the flashlight!" He began to paw through the snow like a dog digging a rabbit out of its hole.

"Milton, what on earth are you doing?"

Milton stopped digging, grabbed the flashlight out of Katie's hand and pointed where he had just dug. "I don't believe it!"

"Milton, what is it?"

"Pavement!" He hurried back to the hole Rudy had fallen down and used the flashlight to sweep away snow. A large chunk fell into the hole, revealing shiny metal.

"Look, Katie! It's a guard rail! Rudy fell right underneath it."

"Rudy!" Katie yelled. Milton joined in. "Rudy!"

Rudy shook his head free from the snow that Milton had inadvertently sent down upon him. He could hear his friends calling him; he just could not answer. Yet if he was to have any hope of rescue, he would have to. Fighting the pain, he took a deep breath. "Help!"

"He's alive!" Katie said.

Milton quickly tied one end of the rope to the post that supported the guard rail. "Rudy!" he yelled, "I'm sending your rope down to you." He threw it far out into the darkness then shone his flashlight downward as leaned out over the guardrail.

"Can you see him?" Katie said.

"No. There's a sharp ledge and then it just drops off."

"Maybe he's hurt. Maybe he can't grab the rope."

Milton wiggled the rope back and forth. "Rudy! Can you see the rope?"

"I think he lost his flashlight," Katie said. "One of us is going to have to go down there and help him."

The very thought made Milton's stomach turn. "Why didn't the stupid jerk watch where he was going?" He had no sooner spoken these words then he realized he spoken out of fear. It scared him to death to think of having to go down into that awful darkness. He was no mountain climber. Furthermore, his hands were numb with cold, and the rope icy slick. "What are we going to do?"

"Maybe you could lower me down on the rope," Katie said.

Milton knew that Katie was suffering from the cold as much, if not more, than he was. There had to be some other way of rescuing Rudy. Milton tried to think what Ramblin' Red might have done in this situation. But Milton was not Ramblin' Red. He lacked Ramblin' Red's courage. Maybe he was just a buttock after all.

"Buttock," Milton whispered.

"What?"

Milton did not answer, for he was thinking of the day he blurted out that word in class, the day Miss Droshky had been lecturing on mechanical advantage. He turned to Katie. "A pulley," he said.

"What about it?"

"A pulley gives mechanical advantage, not only helping to lift a heavy object but to lower it as well."

But he did not have a pulley.

"But, I don't need one!" he yelled. He handed Katie the flashlight then hauled the rope back in. He ran the lead end between his legs, up over one shoulder, back under his arm then once around his wrist before gripping it with his hand. "I can use my body like a pulley! It can act as a brake, supporting my weight."

"Are you sure it will work?"

"Theoretically, it should." That is if he had the courage to test his theory. He heard Ramblin' Red's voice.

Trust your noggin, partner. After all, thinking is what you're good at.

"All right then. Here goes." He stepped over the guard rail and immediately his feet went out from under him. He pulled the rope to his chest and instantly stopped his fall.

"It works!" he exclaimed. Actually, he found it quite easy, even with numb hands and an icy rope. In fact, the slickness of the rope helped to counteract the friction of the rope sliding between his legs and over his shoulder. Slowly, a foot at a time, he lowered himself. "Rudy! I'm coming to get you!"

For Rudy, help could not come too soon. He did not know by what power he still clung to the branch, for he could barely feel the hand that held it. Yet hearing Milton's words gave him the will to hold on a little longer.

Once Milton had descended past the ledge, he was hidden from the light from Katie's flashlight. Yet he could see the reflective tape on Rudy's backpack. "I see you, Rudy!" He moved a step sideways as he continued to descend. Then he was right above Rudy, bracing himself with the rope, and planting his feet lightly in the snow. He dangled the lead end of the rope out in front of Rudy. "Rudy! There's the rope. Grab onto it!"

"I can't!" Rudy managed to croak. "I'm hurt! You've got to tie me off."

"How am I going to do that?

Rudy felt the branch slipping from his fingers. "Milton! I'm slipping! Help me!"

For once, Milton acted without thinking. Had there been time to think about it, he would have realized the advantage he had in being small, for he was able to gain purchase on a slope where Rudy had not been able to. He whipped the rope from around his body, sent the lead end through both straps of Rudy's backpack, hauled in the slack then tied it off, and not an instant too soon, for Rudy lost his grip and went…

Nowhere.

The rope held and kept Rudy from falling, thanks to the sturdy belt that was a part of Rudy's backpack.

"Milton!" Rudy exclaimed, despite his pain. "You did it! You're a regular genius!"

More like a regular idiot, Milton thought. Sure, he had managed to keep Rudy from falling, but he had no idea how he was going to get himself back up, let alone pull Rudy along with him. He racked his brain for a mechanical advantage he might employ in this situation but nothing came to mind, at least not on this end of the rope.

Ramblin' Red spoke again. *Sometimes you've got to use your muscles instead of your brain.*

Ramblin' Red was right. He was just going to have to climb up the slope on his own power and do it now before he lost his nerve as well as all feeling in his fingers.

"Rudy, can you climb at all?"

"I don't think so. I'm sure I busted a rib."

"Here's what I'm going to do. I'm going to climb back up. Then Katie and I can pull you up." He was surprised by how calm he sounded, as if what he purposed was a given fact.

Rudy managed a chuckle. "Okay, I'll just stay here and enjoy the view."

Chapter 32

As Milton went hand over hand up the rope he thought about Ramblin' Red and how, more than ever, he was just a creature of Milton's imagination. Adventures, *real* adventures, at least the type Milton was now undergoing, were a lot more fun to write about than to experience. It made him feel sorry for all the scrapes he had made Ramblin' Red suffer through. Furthermore, no matter how much he admired Ramblin' Red, he could not emulate his courage. Milton wasn't even sure what true courage was. Was he being courageous now? He did not think so. If he were to make it back to the road, it was not because he was courageous, but because he had no other choice; it was either climb back up or let go of the rope and find out just how far he would fall. The latter did not seem a very good option.

The last part of the climb was the hardest, for he had to ascend a nearly vertical wall of icy rock. But Katie, brave soul that she was, had climbed out over the guardrail, and was directing the flashlight so that Milton could see depressions in the rock he could use for toeholds.

"You're a lifesaver, Katie," Milton said when he at last reached the guardrail and hauled himself over it.

Katie continued to point her flashlight downward. "Where's Rudy?"

"He broke a rib. We're going to have to haul him up."

Their task was made easier by having an open end of the guardrail to wrap the rope around as they hauled it in.

"This is really a variation on a simple machine," Milton said. "It's kind of like a wheel and axle where the guardrail is acting as–"

"Milton, please," Katie interrupted, "less talking and more pulling!"

The other factor that lessened their difficulty was Rudy's ability to support most of his own weight. It was only that last section, the wall of rock, that gave them problems.

"Ow!" Rudy howled as Milton and Katie strained on the rope. "You're killing me!"

"Then help us!" Milton called out between breaths. "Use your feet!"

"I'm trying!"

Inch by inch, they gathered in the rope until Rudy's head appeared just below the guardrail. "You don't know how much this hurts," he said.

Milton was past caring how much it hurt. He was exhausted. When they finally hauled Rudy up over the guardrail, both he and Katie fell back onto the snow and lay as two people dead.

Rudy slowly got to his feet. "Somebody shoot me if I ever again decide to go along with one your crazy ideas again, Milton. I mean, if I had wanted to kill myself, I could have jumped out of an airplane without a parachute."

Milton sat up. "Look, Rudy, I'm not the one who couldn't watch where he was going."

"Oh, be quiet, you two!" Katie said. "The important thing is we're safe, and we've found the road."

"We have?" Rudy said.

Milton picked up the flashlight and directed it toward the guardrail. "What do you think that is?"

Rudy looked down the hole he had fallen through. "If this is the section of highway I think it is, I'm lucky to be alive. Indian Creek is like a million miles straight down from here."

"*You're* lucky!" Milton said, standing up. "What about me?"

"We're all of us lucky," Katie said. She tried to stand up but couldn't. "Somebody help me up!"

Because they were so cold and tired, it took both Milton and Rudy to get Katie to her feet.

"How you doing, Katie?" Rudy said.

"I don't know. I've lost all feeling about an hour ago."

"Me, too," Milton said.

"All right, everybody," Rudy said, "group hug."

They stood with arms around each other, trying to get warm. The only sounds were their breathing and the distant roar of Indian Creek.

Milton pushed the snow with his feet. "I thought they were supposed to keep these roads clear."

"They do," Rudy said, "but it takes time, and they usually plow the roads around town first."

"Milton, maybe you better turn your flashlight off," Katie said. "We may need it later."

Without the light, they could not even see each other's faces.

"Are you any warmer, Katie?" Rudy said.

"I'm starting to get some feeling back. How long do you think we'll have to wait until somebody comes by?"

"I don't know."

Milton let out a little laugh.

"What's so funny?" Rudy said.

"If anyone this morning had told me that I'd end the day being hugged by Rudy Kastorsky, I'd have told them they were nuts."

When Rudy did not respond, Milton continued. "Anyway, it beats being slapped on the back of the head and called a buttock."

Rudy cleared his throat. "Okay, I admit it. I've been a…"

"I think the word you're looking for is 'jerk,'" Milton said.

"Well, maybe I *have* been, but it's because smart guys like you always make me feel stupid."

"You're not stupid," Katie said. "Think about your science fair project. Think of all you've done tonight. Where would we have been without you?"

"And I admit I wouldn't mind trading some of my smarts for your wilderness skills," Milton said. "Or to be more patient like you, Katie. The three of us make a good—"

"Quiet!" Rudy commanded.

"What is it?" Milton said.

"Listen! Do you hear that?"

As Milton listened, the noise quickly got louder. "Oh no! It's an avalanche!"

"No!" Katie exclaimed. "I know that sound. It's a snowplow!"

Rudy grabbed the flashlight and directed the light toward the snowplow which suddenly appeared from a bend in the road. "It's my dad!"

Chapter 33

During the winter, Karl Kastorsky worked for the county, driving a big dump truck with a snowplow on the front. The truck had hardly ground to a halt before Karl was out of the cab and marching toward the trio standing in the light of the truck's headlamps.

"Rudy!" Karl yelled "What the hell are you doing here? You're supposed to be staying the night at Grandma's."

"I know, but Miss Droshky was driving along and suddenly there was this big buck—"

"And Miss Droshky tried to not to hit it," Milton said.

"Only the back wheels spun out on the shoulder," Rudy said.

"And went over the embankment, and then—"

"Wait a minute!" Karl yelled. He pointed to the guardrail. "Please, don't tell me the school van went off the road there!"

"No, listen!" Rudy exclaimed. "It went off of the cut-off road. You know, the old logging road and—"

"Which Miss Droshky never should have taken," Milton interrupted.

"What does that matter now?" Rudy said. "The point is—"

"Quiet!" Karl yelled. He turned to Katie. "You look like a level-headed person. Tell me what happened."

Katie tried, but her teeth were chattering too hard.

Karl placed a hand on Katie's shoulder. "Child, you're freezing! How long have you three been out in all this?"

Milton turned his watch to catch the light from the headlamps. "Almost five hours now."

For a moment Karl, did not know what to say. Then he barked an order. "In the truck! The three of you, now!"

They stumbled over to the truck and climbed up into the cab. Katie gave a moan of pleasure, feeling the warmth of the truck's heater.

"I can't tell you how good this heat feels," Rudy said.

Milton held out his hands toward the fan blowing heat. "I thought you said the cold didn't bother you."

"Yeah, well, that was about five hours ago."

Karl got in last, slammed the door and turned on the overhead light. He turned to Katie. "Okay, tell me exactly what happened."

Her voice trembling, Katie explained briefly about the van's accident, about Miss Droshky being hurt, and their deciding to go across country to find help. She got no farther before Karl was on the radio to the highway dispatch.

"Roger that," he said into the handset, "an accident involving school children on forest service road number 1363N."

"My dad knows all the forest road by their numbers," Rudy whispered.

Karl turned to Katie. "Where exactly did the accident happen?"

"I can show you on the map," Milton said. He got his map from his backpack and opened it up. "We went off the road right here," he said, pointing.

Karl looked at the map then spoke into the handset. "Okay, it looks like they went off the road about a half mile west of Keeler pass. The quickest way to get there will be to come in from the east. Likely I'll have to plow our way in, so I'm leaving right now and I'll meet rescue units at the junction of 1363N and the highway. Tell Sheriff Tulles we're going to need at least two ambulances and lots of warm blankets. And make sure the forest service is there just in case the gate's been locked."

Karl replaced the handset and began to turn the truck around. "Okay, you just heard what I said on the radio. But before I do anything I'm going to drop you three off at the school. Your parents must be worried sick, not knowing where you are."

"No way!" Rudy said. "I'm coming with you."

"What about your ribs?" Katie said.

Karl glanced over at Rudy. "What's this about ribs?"

"Ah, it's nothing. I broke a rib. It's just like that time in that game against Westwood."

Karl shook his head. "How do you know you didn't puncture a lung or do damage to your internal organs?"

Rudy began to explain exactly how he knew, giving detailed information about his body temperature, the rib in question and its proximity to internal organs, and his respiratory rate.

"Okay, okay," Karl said, "I believe you, but I'm still taking you all back to the school."

"But you'll need someone to show you the exact location where the van went off the road," Milton said. "It won't be easy to find it, if you don't know exactly where to look."

Karl glanced at Milton. "Aren't you that little kid I chased off my tractor?"

"I'm not a little kid! My name is Milton Mickelsen, and for your information, I'm five feet two inches and growing all the time. But all that doesn't matter. What matters right now is that we get to Miss Droshky and our classmates as quickly as possible. And since it was my idea to find the highway and get help, I'm going with you. I started this whole thing, and I'm going to see it through to the end, and the only way you're going to get me off this truck is to throw me off!"

"That goes for me!" Rudy said.

"And me!" Katie said.

Karl opened his mouth then shut it. Then he began to laugh. "Well, Milton Mickelsen, I'd say you're as feisty as your grandmother. But you're right about finding the van. It would go quicker with you along. Just don't let Marta bite my head off when she asks why I didn't drop all of you off at the school first."

Chapter 34

By the time they got to the junction of forest road 1363N and the main highway, three county sheriff cars, two highway patrol cars, and two ambulances were already there, waiting while a woman from the forest service was unlocking the heavy metal gate that barred the way.

"We couldn't have gotten through this way even if Miss Droshky hadn't run off the road," Milton said.

"I'm surprised the gate was open on the other end," Karl said. "But even with the gate unlocked, your teacher should never have taken this road. I wouldn't be surprised if she loses her job over this."

If she's still alive, Milton thought.

Karl's truck went first past the open gate, the other vehicles following in the path cleared by his snowplow.

"Milton," Karl said, "you're going to have to be my navigator. I figure we got about five miles to the accident site."

Milton consulted his map. "I'd say nearly six."

"Are you sure you can find it? We're coming in from the opposite direction."

"Absolutely!" He pointed to the map. "The van went off the road at the beginning of this long straightaway. It's the only straightaway that goes in the direction of thirty-two degrees, north-northeast." He got out his compass and looked at it. "The compass won't work in here; there's too much metal. But it doesn't matter, the straightaway is just on the other side of the pass."

"Is that how you made your way across country?" Karl said. "With just a map and a compass?"

"We actually had two compasses," Katie said. "I used one. That way we were able to double check our bearings."

"And I went ahead to establish a point we could navigate to," Rudy said.

Karl shook his head. "Unbelievable."

Karl drove as fast as visibility permitted. The plow flung the snow off to one side in a giant white wave. Only at the top of Keeler Pass was he forced to go slow, for there a driving wind hurled snow against the windshield, decreasing visibility.

"Okay," Milton said, "This is the beginning of the long straightaway. The van went off at the far end."

Karl spoke into the handset of his radio, telling those behind that they were almost there.

"There!" cried Milton, Katie and Rudy almost in unison.

Karl brought the truck to a stop, jumped out of the cab and shined his flashlight down the embankment. "Oh, my God!" he exclaimed, seeing the school van smashed up against the tree. Milton, Katie and Rudy started to get out of the truck.

"Get back in there!" Karl yelled. "None of you are to get out of that truck, understood? If I catch one of you out of it, there'll be hell to pay!" Karl turned and joined Sheriff Tulles who was already making his way down the slope. Four other police officers followed along with two ambulance attendants bearing a stretcher.

For a long while, there was nothing for Milton, Katie and Rudy to do but sit in the warm truck cab and speculate about their classmates and Miss Droshky.

"They should be okay," Rudy said. "At least the van is dry and out of the wind."

"What about Miss Droshky?" Katie said.

"The emergency tent is designed to keep in body heat," Rudy said. "And Miss Droshky is kind of fat, and fat acts as a good insulator, keeping a body warm. It's her head injury that worries me."

"Look!" Milton exclaimed. "They're coming back up!"

Anna, Rebecca, and Elizabeth appeared along with two of the police officers. They were immediately bundled in blankets and put into one of the ambulances.

"It looks like they're okay," Rudy said, as they watched the ambulance drive off in the direction they had come.

They had a lot longer to wait before they saw Miss Droshky. Four men appeared, each lifting one corner of the stretcher bearing Miss Droshky. She was strapped into the stretcher with a special strap over her forehead to stabilize her head.

"Look!" Katie exclaimed. "She's talking!"

Milton quickly rolled down the window to hear what she was saying.

"…most wonderful dream. I was floating in warm water under the bluest sky I've ever seen and all around there was a white sandy beach. It must've been Tahiti or someplace just like it." Miss Droshky laid her hand upon the arm of one or her bearers. "You were there, you know, or someone just as handsome."

"Me? In Tahiti?" the stretcher bearer said. "You were dreaming all right." They reached the road and quickly moved toward the rear of the remaining ambulance.

"Well, at least we know she's alive," Milton said, rolling up the window.

The door to the truck opened and Karl leaned in towards them. "Okay, listen up! This is what's going to happen. I've got to stick around here until the tow truck shows up. You three are going back right now with Sheriff Tulles."

"How is everyone?" Milton said, sliding down off the seat.

"How is Miss Droshky?" Katie said.

"They've all got a touch of hypothermia, but they're going to be just fine," Karl said.

Rudy was the last to get out of the truck. "I'd like to stay with you, Dad."

Karl placed a hand on Rudy's shoulder. "You've done enough for one night, son. Now go with the sheriff. I'm sure Grandma is worried."

The three walked toward Sheriff Tulles, who was waiting outside his car.

"Hey!" Karl yelled.

The three turned around.

"You all done good!"

The sheriff opened the back door of his patrol car. "Two of you in the back and one up front."

The back seat was divided from the front by a heavy mesh screen used for isolating offenders. "I'm going to sit back here," Rudy said, as he climbed into the back seat. "Now everyone will think I'm a notorious gangster."

"Why on earth would you want people to think you're a gangster?" Katie said, getting in beside him.

Milton went around and got in the front. The sheriff had kept the engine running, and it was warm inside, almost too warm. The sheriff got into the driver's seat, removed his broad-billed hat and set it on the dashboard. He took time to make notes onto paper attached to a clipboard. Finally, he set the clipboard aside. "Everybody have their seat belts on?"

They assured him they did. The sheriff put on his own seat belt, but made no move to drive off. He turned toward Milton, seated next to him. "Milton, they tell me it was your idea to go across country in a snowstorm to get help."

"Yes, sir," Milton said.

"Well, son," the sheriff said, "that's about the stupidest thing I've ever heard anybody doing!"

Milton was too stunned to reply.

The sheriff held out his hand. "But I'm sure as hell glad you did!"

Milton shook the sheriff's hand. "We all did it. We acted as a team."

The sheriff looked over his shoulder into the back seat. "Well, in my book you're all heroes." He then went on to explain how an earlier truck spill had necessitated closing the highway toward the bottom of the canyon. "Everyone just assumed that the school van had been stuck, waiting for the highway to reopen. By the time we would've figured out otherwise…" He shook his head. "Well, maybe it's best not to think about that. I just know there's going to be a lot of parents mighty grateful for what you've all done this night, not to mention your teacher."

"Maybe she'll give me an A in math," Rudy said.

The sheriff laughed as he put the patrol car in gear. "Now, that might be pushing it a bit, Rudy."

Chapter 35

Sunrise was only a few hours away by the time Marta pulled their truck into the driveway.

"I want you to go straight to bed," Marta said.

"You know today's a school day," Milton said.

"Not for you, it isn't."

Milton was not about to argue. He was exhausted. When the sheriff drove up to the school, it seemed the whole town of Indian Falls was there to greet them. Somehow word had got out about their heroics. The first to greet Milton was his grandmother who hugged him so hard he thought he might end up with a broken rib like Rudy. Then it seemed everyone wanted to shake his hand. The local reporter even asked for an interview.

"Rupert!" Marta told the reporter, "if you know what's good for you, you'll leave the boy alone. Right now, he needs his bed." The reporter acquiesced, but not before taking a photo of the three heroes.

Milton tramped up the stairs to his bedroom. Yet when he got into bed, he could not sleep. He tried reading a new sci-fi novel, for reading sometimes helped him nod off, but all he could think about was what he and his companions had gone through, which got him thinking about Ramblin' Red. Having come through his own ordeal, Milton felt he could not leave Ramblin' Red dangling, half dead, half alive. He got out of bed, went to his desk and took up his pencil.

The days spent in recovery would live forever in Ramblin' Red's memory. Each afternoon Dr. Sutcliffe came to visit him. The doctor was no sooner through the door of Stark's cabin before Ramblin' Red posed the same question: Had the posse managed to catch Kid Torkasky? Each time he received the same answer: Not yet.

As Ramblin' Red regained his strength, he and the doctor went for walks together. Randy Stark had chosen a beautiful spot to homestead. The land backed up against a high sandstone mesa, which provided welcome afternoon shade. In the other direction, the broad Pecos River snaked through the valley outlined by shimmering cottonwood trees. Stark had channeled water from a nearby spring to irrigate a large vegetable garden. For want of something to do, Ramblin' Red weeded the garden alongside Stark's boys. It was an occupation foreign to him, yet it gave him great satisfaction and recalled to him the dream he had had. The boys had taken a shining to Ramblin' Red, and eagerly awaited the evenings when Ramblin' Red would fill their ears with tales of his rambles or teach them cowboy skills.

One afternoon, the boys asked Ramblin' Red if they might go fishing. They were honest, hard-working boys, always conscientious about doing their chores, and Ramblin' Red thought they deserved a break from the hard work of homesteading. Gathering up their fishing poles, the boys rode away toward the river, two upon Cricket and two upon a decrepit old mare that Stark kept around, mostly out of kindness. Thus it was that Dr. Sutcliffe found Ramblin' Red alone when she arrived that day. Out of habit they began to walk along the path that led to the mesa.

"How are you feeling?" Dr. Sutcliffe said.

Ramblin' Red stretched one arm over his head. "Outside of being a mite stiff, I'm fit as a fiddle."

Dr. Sutcliffe smiled. "It seems my patient is cured, and that means I'll no longer need to pay him visits."

Ramblin' Red clutched his side and fell to his knees in the soft sand.

"Max! What is it?"

"I don't know. When you said that about not visiting, I suddenly got this great pain in my side. I think I may be having one of them relapses."

"Oh, phooey!" she exclaimed, and, stealing his hat, she ran up the pathway, laughing.

Ramblin' Red caught up with her at the base of the mesa. The doctor played hard to get, dodging around boulders and staying just out of Ramblin' Red's reach. Then she zigged when she should have zagged, and Ramblin' Red caught her about the waist. He held her tight for one divine moment before releasing her and picking up his hat, which she had dropped. When he straightened up, Dr. Sutcliffe was pinning back loose strands of hair.

"What?" she said, in response to the strange look Ramblin' Red gave her.

A little red in the face, Ramblin' Red turned away. "Sorry, but seeing you tidying up your hair like that reminded me of that dream I had about us."

Dr. Sutcliffe sat upon a natural bench formed of sandstone and motioned for Ramblin' Red to join her. "So, tell me about this dream of yours."

Ramblin' Red took off his hat and idly ran his fingers around the brim as he told her about the field of corn, the white clapboard house and her standing in the field alongside him, pinning up her hair. "I can't seem to get that dream out of my head," he said, putting his hat back on.

"Why's that?"

"Well, I've never thought about being a farmer. I've never thought about being anything, really. I've always just rambled around, taking things as they come, one day at a time."

"Which is the way you've always loved to live your life."

Ramblin' Red looked into her violet-blue eyes. "Is it?"

"What are you trying to say, Max?"

He turned and stared at the valley spread out before them. "I know I lack certain refinements. I certainly don't have a whole lot of formal education like you. But I know what is true, and the truth is there's no one who could love you more than I do, and there's no one who would work harder to make you happy." He got down on one knee before her. "So what I'm trying to say is this: Laura Sutcliffe, will you marry me?"

The question really did not come as a surprise. It seems they had been moving toward this from the very first time they had met.

"Aren't you supposed to take your hat off when you propose marriage?" she said.

When Ramblin' Red removed his hat, she leaned forward and planted a kiss on his forehead then cradled his face in her hands. "You don't need to work harder to make me happy. You just need to be who you are." Then she kissed him full on the lips.

It was the kiss that Ramblin' Red would remember the most. He had kissed and been kissed many a time, but this was the first time a kiss ever meant anything. "I'll take that as a yes," Ramblin' Red said, when they parted.

"Yes, Max," she said. "Yes, I will marry you."

He leaped up, lifted her up off her feet and spun her around in circles.

"Oh!" she cried. "I'm getting dizzy!"

He set her down, took her hand and together they ran back along the trail.

"Where are we going?" she said.

"I don't know, but I just got to tell somebody the good news!"

Laughing, they ran on until they came around a bend to find three armed gunmen blocking their way.

Chapter 36

"Well, if this don't beat all!" Kid Torkasky declared, training one of his pearl-handled pistols on Ramblin' Red. Beside him were two of his henchmen, one of whom was slumped forward, dripping blood onto his saddle. "And here I've been thinking it's been a pretty lousy day." Kid Torkasky's earlier attempt to rob the Stockmans Bank had been foiled when an unruly student, forced to stay after school to write sentences on the board, had spied the three desperados sneaking into town by the back way. The boy had run to warn the deputy who Sheriff Roswell had appointed in his absence. The deputy, a better shot than the sheriff, managed to wing one of the robbers before the three made their escape.

Ramblin' Red raised up his hands. "I'm unarmed, Kid. So, what is it you want?"

The Kid pointed his pistol at Dr. Sutcliffe. "What I want right now is the doctor."

Ramblin' Red immediately stepped in front of her. "You'll leave her alone!"

The Kid grinned. "Now, now, there ain't no need to get all riled up. I just need for her to take a look at Rufus here." He gestured toward the wounded rider. "He seems to have gotten himself in the way of a bullet."

When Ramblin' Red did not move, the Kid raised his pistol until the barrel was pointed right at Ramblin' Red's head. "Now, you can stand there playing the hero while I shoot you, or you can step aside and let the doctor do her job!"

"Please, Max," Laura said, "let me do as he says."

With great reluctance, Ramblin' Red stepped aside.

If Dr. Laura Sutcliffe was afraid, she did not show it. "You'll need to get

Rufus into the cabin if I'm to help him."

The Kid ordered his other henchman to help get Rufus inside. When all three disappeared into the cabin, the Kid slowly dismounted, still keeping his pistol trained on Ramblin' Red. "Put your hands on your head and turn around!" When Ramblin' Red obeyed, the Kid placed the barrel of his pistol in the middle of Ramblin' Red's back. "Now march back up the way you came and don't try any funny business, or I'll shoot you right here in sight of your sweetheart."

"I don't know how you've come to live so long, Kid," Ramblin' Red said as he marched along. "I'd have thought by now someone would've shot you in a place where it would've done some good."

Ramblin' Red's allusion to the Kid's getting shot in the buttock was still a literal sore spot with the Kid. "You've been dogging me ever since that time I was herding a few steers down along the border."

"That's because the steers you were herding didn't belong to you."

"Ha! The way I see it, finders, keepers."

"So, what are you going to do now, shoot me in the back like the coward you are?"

The Kid jabbed Ramblin' Red with his pistol. "I'd watch my tongue, if I were you. I'm planning to kill you nice and quick, but I can make it long and ugly if you like."

When they reached the base of the mesa, the Kid ordered Ramblin' Red to stop. "Now, turn around!"

Ramblin' Red turned.

"Any last words before I send you to meet your maker?"

"Can I put my hands down? This is getting right uncomfortable."

The Kid nodded. "Anything else?"

Ramblin' Red stared up at the sheer face of red sandstone towering directly above him then back to the kid. "Well, I thought about calling you a dirty dog, but it didn't seem right to be so objectionable on such pretty day like this."

As the Kid took aim, Ramblin' Red saw his life flash before his eyes. He recalled the first time he had seen Cricket running free on the Colorado plains. He saw the majestic mountains and fertile valleys he and Cricket had wandered through. There were the faces of friends he had made and would miss.

But mostly he saw Laura Sutcliffe and the life that now they would never share.

"I've been looking forward to this for a long time," the Kid said.

But the Kid never got the chance to pull the trigger. From above him came a terrifying shriek.

The Kid looked up. "What the—" which were the last words he uttered before Miss Droshky, the schoolmarm, launched out of the back of her runaway wagon, landed on Kid Torkasky and smashed him flat.

There was no time for Ramblin' Red to consider how it was he had been saved in such an unlikely manner, nor to determine who the woman was whose timely arrival had given him life. He grabbed the pistol that had fallen out of Kid Torkasky's hand and raced back down the trail. But when he arrived at Stark's cabin he found it ringed by the sheriff's posse. Then the two outlaws, hands above their heads, emerged from the cabin, followed by Sheriff Roswell, gun in hand, followed by Dr. Laura Sutcliffe.

"Max!" Laura cried, seeing Ramblin' Red. She ran into his arms "Oh, Max, Max, I was sure the Kid was going to shoot you."

"He was! He almost did!"

She looked into his eyes. "But you're here! You're alive!" Which begged the question of how?

"I was saved by an angel," he said. "A rather fat angel, but the point is a celestial being descended from the heavens to save me."

Laura leaned her head against his chest. "Oh, Max how many times will I live, thinking I have lost you?"

"Never again!" he assured her. "Even if it means we'll have to move into another story."

There was a shuffling sound, and the lovers turned to see Miss Droshky, looking a lot wider in one direction and thinner in the other, weaving her way down the trail toward them. She stopped in the path to do her interpretation of the hula-hula.

"Oh, I love to sit by the sandy bay, where the dolphins swim and the palm trees sway," Miss Droshky sang, swinging her hips and waving her arms side to side. Then she came forward, shoved Laura out of the way and proceded to start unbuttoning Ramblin' Red's shirt. "All my beaus have bare chests!" she declared.

Laura Sutcliffe looked confused. "Max, who is this woman?"

Ramblin' Red, busy trying to button the buttons Miss Droshky kept unbuttoning, tried to explain. "This is the angel I was telling you about, the one who saved me from Kid Torkasky."

"Angel!" Laura cried, looking a little piqued.

Fortunately, Sheriff Roswell arrived to take control of the situation. "Miss Droshky," he said, taking Miss Droshky by the hand, "have you been at Shorty's whiskey again, because you're sure acting like it?"

"Oh, hey handsome!" Miss Droshky cried, putting her arm around the sheriff's waist. "You wouldn't happen to own a sail boat, would you?"

Sheriff Roswell looked at Ramblin' Red and Laura. "Don't worry, folks. She'll be okay once she has a chance to sleep it off." The sheriff began to lead Miss Droshky away. "C'mon, Miss Droshky."

Ramblin' Red and Laura watched as Miss Droshky, along with the sheriff, posse and prisoners–hands tied to the horns of their saddles–rode off in the direction of Pandemonium.

"Remember your promise," Laura said, leaning her head upon Ramblin' Red's shoulder. "Don't make me have to think I've lost you again."

Ramblin' Red put his arms around her. Yet as he watched the riders disappear in the distance, he wondered about how a person's life gets written, and whether it was a promise he would be able to keep.

Chapter 37

"The Stainless Steel Rat is great," Rudy said, leading the way uphill though the forest, "but I like Alex Rider even better."

"What's he talking about?" Katie said, following along behind Rudy.

"You haven't read the Alex Rider series?" Milton said, bringing up the rear.

"I've never even heard of them," Katie said.

"That's because you're a girl," Rudy said. "You wouldn't like them. There's no damsels swooning into the arms of some big-lipped baboon."

"Rudy," Katie said, "if your backpack wasn't in the way, I'd kick you in the you-know-what."

"Buttock!" Rudy and Milton chimed in unison, then laughed.

"Hey!" Rudy exclaimed, topping the ridge, "there's Round Lake!"

Milton consulted his compass. "Just where it's supposed to be."

The three friends stood alongside each other and looked down at the lake. Rudy adjusted a shoulder strap on his backpack then wiped the sweat from his forehead with the back of his sleeve. "Man, it's hot!"

"I'll take heat over snow any day," Katie said.

Milton and Rudy, remembering last winter's adventure, voiced their agreement.

"At least it's cooler up here than down at our cabin," Milton said. "Grandma thinks we're in for a hot summer."

"Well, we won't be hot once we're in the lake," Rudy said. He began to run down the hill. "C'mon, last one in is a big-lipped baboon!"

It was hard running with bulky backpacks, and they were hot and sweaty by the time they reached the lake. They leaned their backpacks up against the same cedar tree that had sheltered Milton and Mr. Cunningham during the thunderstorm last fall. As they sat on the ground, resting, Milton pulled a rumpled letter out of his backpack.

"You've been hauling that letter around all week," Rudy said. "What's in it?"

"It's from the writing contest I entered," Milton said.

"Was that the one on the poster in the hall at school?" Katie said.

Milton nodded.

"Well, aren't you curious what it says?" Rudy said.

"Of course. It's just that I don't take rejection very well."

"How do you know you didn't win?" Katie said.

"Hey!" Rudy exclaimed, "speaking of writing, did you hear Miss Droshky got a whole lot of money for that book she wrote?"

It seemed everyone had heard about the advance Miss Droshky had received for her soon-to-be-published romance.

"I hear she's moving to Hawaii," Katie said.

"The moon wouldn't be far enough," Rudy said. "I'm still surprised they let her keep her job after what happened."

Milton tapped the edge of the letter against the palm of his hand. It irked him that Miss Droshky could get published by writing what he considered to be drivel.

"So you gonna open that letter or what?" Rudy said.

Milton slowly tore open the envelope and removed its contents.

"Read it to us," Katie said.

Milton cleared his throat then began to read.

" 'Dear Mr. Mickelsen. Thank you for your entry in the 37th annual writing contest sponsored by The Association of School Principals and the Association of School Superintendents. We were pleased by the great response we received to this year's theme, *Why I write*. Unfortunately, your essay was not chosen to receive one of the prizes. Please note that the number of prizes awarded was small in comparison to the number of entries received, and many excellent essays did not receive prizes.

" 'We urge you not to be discouraged. Good writing takes time, and by participating in our contest, you have already shown you're on your way to becoming a good writer.

" 'We look forward to reading your entry into next year's contest. The theme will be: *The Writer's Journey: My Goal as a Writer.*

" 'Thank you again for your participation.

" 'Sincerely, the Association of School Superintendents.' "

Milton crumpled up the paper and threw it in the nearby fire pit.

"I'm sorry you didn't win anything, Milton," Rudy said. He stood up. "Well, I'm going swimming. You two want to come?"

"In a minute," Katie said. She waited while Rudy got his swim trunks out of his backpack then went in search of a place to change clothes. "Don't look so sad, Milton. It's just one contest. There'll be others."

"I'm just a little disappointed, that's all," Milton said, drawing figures in the dirt with a stick. "I know there are lots of famous writers who got lots of rejection letters before being published."

"Sometime I'd like to read your essay," Katie said.

"I have it right here, actually."

"Would you care to read it to me?"

Milton got out his writing pad, which contained the final draft of his essay.

" 'Why I Write, by Milton Mickelsen.

Many writers have said that they write in order to make sense of their lives, and to some degree that is true for me.' "

He looked up. "I think I should have written 'extent' instead of 'degree.' "

"Keep reading, Milton."

He returned to his paper. " 'I think the truth is, no matter how much I write, life will never make complete sense. Life is too uncertain. There are too many variables. No one can predict what will happen in life, so how can a writer say he can make sense of what is unpredictable? Rather than say, "I write to make sense of my life," a writer should say, "Only in writing does life make any sense," for the writer is privileged to have command over life's variables, to order life as he would like it. This is not to say that writing is always predictable. When I write, there is a voice inside my head telling me a story, and often what the voice says comes as a complete surprise to me. These revelations are actually what makes writing fun. That said, it is I and not the voice in my head that has the final say. I determine what gets put down on paper.

" 'This last winter, my friends and I had what might be called an adventure. Guided by map and compass, we went across country in a snowstorm to get help after the van we were traveling in crashed in a remote wilderness area. It was the kind of experience that would make for exciting reading, yet I have never written about it. Why? I am not certain, and this troubles me. But I believe the answer has something to do with the difference between life and writing. I enjoy reading adventures; I enjoy writing them. But my experience in a real-life adventure proved to be anything but enjoyable. In fact, at times it was terrifying. That is because life is not like writing; if it was, I would never pick up a pencil again.

" 'But I will because I am a writer. And, for me, it is not a requirement that my writing make sense of life. My only requirement is to write down the stories spoken by the voice inside my head.' "

Milton set his writing pad down. "So, what do you think?"

"I think it's good," Katie said. "But I'm a little confused."

"In what way?"

"Well, don't you think you can draw from your experiences to make your writing more realistic?"

Milton nodded. "I thought of that. But I don't know that I want to make my writing more realistic. I mean, Ramblin' Red, the character in the book I've been writing, is a kind of a superhero; he does things that really can't be done, and I like that."

"But that makes Ramblin' Red a comic book character. Real people aren't like that. I would think that you would want your writing to be more true to life."

"You sound like Grandma. She talks about me finding my own voice. Like I wrote in my essay, I already have a voice. I call him Walt and he lives inside my head and tells me stories. I figure when Walt is ready for me to write more realistically, he'll start telling me more realistic stories. In the meantime, I'm not ready to give up on Ramblin' Red."

"That's okay by me," Katie said, standing up. "Ready for a swim?"

"I'll catch up a little later. I want to do a little writing first."

As Katie went off to change into a bathing suit, Milton stared at the essay he had written. "I don't know why I write," he said. "I just do." He turned the page on his writing pad and took up his pencil.

Ramblin' Red and Laura Sutcliffe were married on a day in June when the cottonwood trees along the Pecos River were leafy green. So many people wanted to attend the wedding ceremony that it had to be held outside. Sheriff Roswell gave the bride away, while Nero Marceau acted as best man.

Following a brief honeymoon, camping out in nearby mountains, the married couple moved into in a small rental in Pandemonium while Ramblin' Red looked for property suitable for a farm. Because Laura's practice necessitated her being close to town, Ramblin' Red could not take advantage of lands available under the Homestead Act, but over the years, he had set aside money, and with it he was able to purchase forty acres along the Pecos River not far from town.

Then came the work of making his dream a reality. Ramblin' Red hired out on several cattle drives and chose to receive his wages in cattle. Eventually, he had enough cattle that with the proceeds from the yearling sales, he was able to start building a house on their land.

The construction of the house took time, for Ramblin' Red wanted the white clapboard house to be just like the one in his dream. Laura said it was worth the wait, for when the house was finished, it was all they had hoped for. Still, it looked lonely, sitting all by itself in an open field. So Ramblin' Red and Laura took cuttings from the river cottonwoods to plant alongside it. The cottonwoods quickly grew to shade the house and the green lawns surrounding the house, and when the time came, provided their children with trees to climb.

With the death of Kid Torkasky and the incarceration of his henchmen, things settled down in Pandemonium, New Mexico. More and more families were moving into the area, and that meant schools and churches were being built, and these developments had a civilizing effect. People began to wonder if the name Pandemonium seemed appropriate anymore.

Thus, it was that when after many years of dedicated service Sheriff Frank Roswell finally passed away, it seemed fitting to change the town's name to Roswell. As the town of Roswell grew, so did Laura's practice until she was forced to take on first one assistant then another, and there was talk of building a hospital. As Laura's practice prospered, so did the farm.

During the long summer evenings, Ramblin' Red and Laura would often walk hand in hand through their orchard while their children played hide and seek in amongst the tall fruit trees. In seeing all that had been accomplished, Ramblin' Red felt the satisfaction that comes from having a dream fulfilled. This did not mean he still did not have the urge to ramble. Yet when the urge became too strong, he would simply load up the buckboard, and he and Laura and the children would spend a week or two in those majestic mountains he had wandered through in his younger days. And though Ramblin' Red might have missed some of his adventures, he would not have traded his new life for all the adventures to be had in the world. For there, along the meandering Pecos River, Ramblin' Red found true happiness, and he and Laura and their children lived in peace and contentment…

…until they were all abducted by aliens.

www.ingramcontent.com/pod-product-compliance
Lightning Source LLC
Chambersburg PA
CBHW082010170626
46817CB00009B/3047